The Trail
of the
Chocolate
Thief

**Other Scholastic books by
James Heneghan:**

(about the O'Brien Detective Agency)
The Case of the Marmalade Cat

(with Bruce McBay as B.J. Bond)
Goodbye, Carlton High

Blue

The Trail of the Chocolate Thief

JAMES HENEGHAN

Cover by
Janet Wilson

Scholastic Canada Ltd.

Scholastic Canada Ltd.
123 Newkirk Road, Richmond Hill, Ontario, Canada L4C 3G5

Scholastic Inc.
730 Broadway, New York, NY 10003, USA

Ashton Scholastic Limited
Private Bag 1, Penrose, Auckland, New Zealand

Ashton Scholastic Pty Limited
PO Box 579, Gosford, NSW 2250, Australia

Scholastic Publications Ltd.
Villiers House, Clarendon Avenue, Leamington Spa
Warwickshire CV32 5PR, UK

Canadian Cataloguing in Publication Data

Heneghan, James, 1930-
    The trail of the chocolate thief

ISBN 0-590-74514-X

I. Title.

PS8565.E54T7 1993   jC813'.54   C93-093667-1
PZ7.H45Tr 1993

6 5 4 3 2 1   Printed in Canada   3 4 5 6 /9

For Lee Michael — welcome to the world.

Chapter 1

"Christmas is my favourite time of year," said Sadie Stewart with a sigh of pleasure. "Santa Claus, and love and peace . . ."

"Take your feet off my desk," said Clarice O'Brien.

". . . and good will toward men," Sadie finished with a glare at her friend.

"Feet?" said Clarice gently. Patience didn't come easily to her; she had to work at it.

"Even TV commercials don't spoil it," said Sadie. "Christmas is unspoilable."

"Sadie! Do you mind?"

"The only thing that almost spoils it," said Sadie, "is the rain. Vancouver is the umbrella capital of the world: it's always raining, especially at Christmastime. Just once in my life I'd like to see a white Christmas. Wouldn't you like to see a white Christmas before you die, Clarice?"

It was Saturday afternoon, the first day of the holiday, five days to Christmas, and the two friends were relaxing in the garden shed where Mr. O'Brien kept all his tools and seeds and clay pots. The sign on the outside of the shed said

O'BRIEN DETECTIVE AGENCY
NO JOB TOO BIG OR TOO SMALL
CLARICE O'BRIEN, PROP.

The sign could be clearly seen by anyone passing in the back lane.

Outside it was raining.

Clarice sat at the potting table, which had been cleared to make a desk under the window. On the desk was a small notebook, a blue plastic pencil holder containing several sharp pencils, a desk calendar, and a magnifying glass that had a slight chip out of its lower edge near the handle. There were two wooden chairs, old and scarred.

Sadie was slumped in the client chair to the side of the desk, her feet in their wet runners propped up on the desk. She was polishing her glasses with a square of soft cloth she always carried with her for that purpose. She was a year younger than Clarice.

"I don't know about a white Christmas," said Clarice with enormous effort, "but what I would like to see is your muddy runners off my desk."

"You could say please."

"Please."

Sadie swung her feet down off the desk. "Seems to me you've got something on your mind. You've been crabby for days. This constant rain can do that to people, make them crabby and difficult. My mother, for example —"

"I'm not crabby!" snapped Clarice.

"What's on your mind, then?" asked Sadie, undaunted.

"My Aunt Esther is coming to stay with us over Christmas, and she's bringing her kid. I'm sure to get the job of babysitting her for the whole holiday." Clarice made a face.

"How old is she?"

"Seven. Her mother is as loopy as banana jam."

"What's her name?"

"Esther."

"Not your aunt." Sadie rolled her eyes. "Your cousin!"

"Moonflower."

Sadie's brown eyes widened. "That's her name? Moonflower?"

"I told you my aunt is loopy. She's loopier than a fish."

"A moon child," mused Sadie, "born on the moon, or under the moon. A flower child, born in a meadow, or perhaps . . ."

"She was born in Horsefly," said Clarice, cutting short her friend's flight of poetical fancy. "It's way up north someplace. My Aunt Esther teaches school there."

"Moonflower is a good name," Sadie decided. "I like it much better than my name. Sadie sounds old-fashioned and stuffy. Makes much more sense to have a name like Moonflower; it's poetic and really means something."

"My name is poetic and really means something," said Clarice; "it means . . . "

"I already know what it means, Clarice."

". . . bright and shining," continued Clarice, "and having the power to see things other people can't see. . . ."

Sadie gave a huge sigh of boredom.

"I call them Hunches," Clarice finished. "It's a kind of sixth sense."

"Which is why you will be a world-famous detective some day," said Sadie sarcastically. "I've heard it so many times I know it by heart. I wake in the middle of the night singing it to the tune of 'Jingle Bells'!"

Clarice said nothing but turned her head away to stare out the shed window.

"Brick's late," said Sadie. Brick, the third member of the agency, was usually late, for his sense of time came from some internal rhythm all his own.

Silence. Clarice continued staring out the window.

"I'm sorry, Clarice," said Sadie. "My major resolution come New Year is no more sarcasm. I like your name. I like it a heap better than Sadie. And you really will be a famous detective one day, I know it."

"Isn't it a bit early for New Year's resolutions?" said Clarice stiffly.

"I need to practise."

Clarice stood and stretched. The rain fell steadily on the O'Briens' neat backyard and on the Fairview Slopes and all over Vancouver. "It's so wet out there; maybe Brick won't come today."

"What's Moonflower like?"

Clarice watched the rain. "I haven't seen her for years, but all seven-year-olds are a nuisance, everyone knows that. She'll get in the way."

There was a soft bump outside the garden shed.

"Here comes Brick," said Clarice.

The door swung open. The two girls turned and fixed their attention on the open doorway. They waited expectantly.

Brick, rain glistening on his wild face like war paint, suddenly exploded through the doorway in a high leap and landed in a crouch facing the desk. His open hands slashed at the air like fan blades. "Aieee!" he screamed.

Sadie rolled her eyes. "It's the spirit of Christmas himself, vibrating with peace and good will!"

Brick grinned. "Any cases, Chief?" he said to Clarice. In contrast to his killer yell, he spoke quietly, as though talking were an effort.

"Nothing yet, Number Three," answered Clarice, "but I'm expecting one any minute. I have a Hunch. Christmas is a busy time for criminals."

Brick stared at her unblinkingly for a few seconds with his strange amber eyes under their yellow lashes. He was a thin boy with spiky yellow hair. In spite of the rain on his face there was a sun-baked, tawny look to him; his skin was covered in freckles the same colour as his eyes.

He turned lithely and leaped onto the top of a high pile of seed potatoes in hessian sacks where he stretched and yawned and then settled himself comfortably. He blinked lazily down at the two girls with sleepy eyes. Brick rarely spoke. His main usefulness as a detective was his astonishing athletic ability, for when it came to climbing rooftops and squeezing through windows Brick was worth his weight in ice cream.

Sadie leaned back in her chair and propped her feet back up on Clarice's desk.

"Number Two? Please? You're doing it again."

"You're not supposed to call me Number Two unless we're on a case," Sadie reminded her.

"Feet off the desk!" Clarice snapped.

Sadie pretended not to hear. "What I like most about Christmas," she said, "is the thought of all those little kids waiting for Santa Claus to climb down their chimneys with toys."

Clarice's face was quite red.

"Santa Claus doesn't actually need to crawl down chimneys to spread Christmas cheer and good will," continued Sadie easily. "All he needs to do is wave his hand and perform a miracle."

"Huh?" said Clarice, her anger now mixed with disbelief. "Don't tell me you still believe in Santa Claus!" she hooted.

"Of course I do," said Sadie. "Santa Claus is real, everyone knows that. Saint Nicholas is his proper name, of course. You just pronounce it a little differently and it's Santa Claus." Sadie read a lot and was smart. She was also a know-it-all.

"That stuff is for kids, Sadie."

Sadie slid her feet off the desk. "It's for

everyone, Clarice, not just kids. St. Nicholas is the one who spreads all that Christmas spirit. How else can you explain why everyone feels so good at this time of year? And he's especially busy taking care of the poor and helping the lame and the crippled, and curing the sick."

Clarice stared at her friend in astonishment. Then she shook her head. "Some people might think you're loopy for believing all that stuff, Sadie, loopier even than my Aunt Esther. But as your best friend I gotta overlook it and try to think of you as trusting and positive."

"Thanks for the compliment," said Sadie sarcastically. But she looked pleased.

"What about you, Number Three?" Clarice directed her voice toward the top of the potato sacks. "Do you still believe in Santa Claus?"

"Huh?" said Brick sleepily.

"Do you believe in Santa Claus?" Clarice repeated.

Brick frowned with the effort of thinking. Except for a small sigh from Sadie, the girls waited patiently. At last, Brick's amber eyes lit up with wakefulness and intelligence. "Sure I believe in claws." He held up his hands, showing their little pointed fingernails. "They should be kept clean and sharp, always at the ready." He grinned happily down at them. Then he gave a wide, slow, gaping yawn that revealed two perfect rows of straight white teeth.

The girls stared. Brick lay down again and closed his eyes.

Sadie looked at Clarice. In her very best sarcastic manner she said, "I'd almost swear sometimes that Number Three is human!"

"Brick is a good detective," said Clarice. "That's all that matters."

But Sadie was no longer interested in Brick. She turned her head sharply toward the door. "What's that?" she said.

 **Chapter 2**

"What's what?" asked Clarice. Sadie craned her neck so that her slightly prominent ears, usually hidden by her long hair, pointed toward the door like satellite dishes.

"I hear someone crying," said Sadie.

Clarice listened but could hear nothing. "It's those sensitive ears of yours, Number Two; they're picking up the skiers on Grouse Mountain bellyaching about the lack of snow."

"It's someone crying," insisted Sadie.

Clarice listened again. "All I hear is the rain on the roof. Your Superior Hearing Equipment has blown a fuse."

There was a tiny knock on the door.

"Told you so," said Sadie.

Clarice got up and opened it. A little girl in a hooded, bright fluorescent green-and-pink jacket stood outside in the rain looking up at Clarice with tearful dark eyes.

"Come in and sit down, kid." Clarice pointed to the client chair. Sadie got up and steered the little girl to the chair, loosening the hood around her face.

"What's your name?" said Clarice.

The child sniffled and snuffled with grief.

Sadie pulled a book from her jacket pocket. She reached down farther, located a wad of tissue that was only slightly used, and applied it to the end of the child's red nose. "It's Wendy Wakabayashi," she explained to Clarice. "She lives near me in the Creek."

Brick sat up and watched the scene sleepily through half-closed eyes.

"Somebody stealed my baby," sniffed Wendy, her tears diminishing under Sadie's motherly mopping.

"Your baby?" said Clarice. "You mean your doll?"

Wendy nodded. "Her name is Belinda Misty. She was fast asleep with baby Jesus and somebody stealed her."

Clarice turned to Sadie. "What's all this baby Jesus stuff?"

"The Wakabayashis have a Christmas nativity scene in their front yard," explained Sadie, "with painted figures of Jesus, Mary and Joseph, and the shepherd and the three wise kings."

Clarice turned back to the little girl. "Did baby Jesus get stolen, too? Or any of the other people?"

Wendy shook her head. "Only Belinda Misty."

"What does Belinda Misty look like?" asked Clarice.

Wendy sniffled. "She's a Cabbage Patch Kid and she's got blue eyes and red hair and freckles just like you and and she's almost a year old and I adopted her on the thirteenth of April and I'm her mother and this is her birth 'tificate." She plonked a scrap of paper down on the desk in front of Clarice. "And somebody stealed her."

"Kidnapped," growled Brick.

Clarice turned to Sadie. "You get all that?" Sadie nodded. She was secretary as well as Detective Number Two.

"Wendy, did you see anyone take it?" said Clarice. Wendy shook her head. "Did anyone else see it taken?" Another shake. "Do you have any idea who might have taken it?" No.

Clarice said earnestly, "Well, we'll do our best to find Belinda Misty for you. But we make no promises; dolls are like people, they go missing sometimes. The fee is . . . " She stopped and thought. "If we find your doll it will cost three chocolate bars."

Wendy nodded solemnly.

Just then the door flew open and in rushed a girl who whipped off her bright green rain hat and shook it fiercely, sending a shower over Wendy. Wendy jumped from her chair, edged herself around the new arrival, and hurried away out the door.

The new girl had a lazy, superior smile. "Are you O'Brien?"

"Clarice," said Clarice. "Come in and sit down." She introduced Sadie and Brick. "Sadie is our secretary," she explained.

"*Detective*-secretary," said Sadie.

The girl had green eyes and pale skin, and her hair was fine and yellow and long. She wore a green raincoat that matched her hat. She unzipped her fanny pack, reached in, pulled out a telephone, and punched a number with her finger. Then she put the phone to her ear.

"I'm at O'Brien's," she said to the person at the other end. "Should only be here a few minutes. . . . Yes. . . . G'bye." She pushed the telephone back inside her pack, but didn't sit. Instead, she stood, smiling down at Clarice with green-eyed superiority.

During the girl's telephone performance,

Clarice and Sadie had been staring at her with a great deal of astonishment and awe. "It was like being visited by '60 Minutes'," Sadie said later.

"That's one of those — er — cellular phones isn't it?" said Clarice, who was playing for time while she regained her composure.

"I can see why you're a detective," said the girl. "You don't miss anything, do you?" She reached into her pack again, extracted a chocolate bar, tore off its wrapper, and tossed it carelessly onto the floor. "Chocolate, anyone?"

"No thanks," said Clarice, "we're On Duty. What can we do for you?"

"My mountain bike. It's a Horwood. Stolen. I'm quite annoyed. Find it and there's a fifty in it for you."

"A fifty!" said Sadie. Her eyes widened.

Clarice launched her interrogation. "What's your name?"

"Priscilla Charles."

"Where was the bicycle stolen from?"

"Porch. 648 The Castings. That's in False Creek."

"Was the bicycle locked?"

"Of course it wasn't locked! If it were locked I wouldn't be here now, would I? It wouldn't be stolen, would it?"

Clarice struggled to keep a professional composure. "Did you see anyone around, anyone suspicious?"

Priscilla rolled her eyes to the roof. "Are all these questions really necessary? No, I didn't."

"When did you discover it missing?"

"This morning after breakfast, about ten o'clock."

"When did you last see your bike?"

"Last night about nine o'clock, I suppose. I left it outside on the porch."

"What colour is it?"

The girl's laugh was a cool tinkle, like ice in a glass. "What, the porch?"

Clarice was losing her patience. She glared at the girl. "The bike!"

Priscilla shrugged. "What a bore! Let me think. Er — black and blue."

"You don't seem too sure."

"It's your questions. They're so tiresome."

"I think that should be enough for now," said Clarice, trying not to snarl. "Leave your phone number with Sadie in case we need to contact you."

Priscilla Charles scribbled a number in Sadie's notebook, gave Brick a steady, lingering smile, pulled her rain hat down over her ears, and strutted to the door. She looked back. "Ciao!

It was a slice meeting you all." She winked at Brick. The door closed behind her.

Clarice raked her fingers through her hair as though ridding herself of cobwebs.

"I know her," said Sadie. "She's president of the school Debating Club."

Clarice looked grim. "It's just as I thought, Number Two. I had a Hunch we'd have an Important Case before Christmas."

Chapter 3

"This promises to be a most interesting Case," said Clarice, drumming her lower lip with the eraser end of her pencil.

It was the next morning, Sunday. Outside it was all puddles and promises: the rain had finally stopped, and here and there a patch of blue showed through the heavy grey clouds.

"A doll and a mountain bike," said Sadie, looking up from her book, *Tales of Merrie England*. "Looks to me like two cases, not one."

"What do you mean?" said Clarice.

"I think it's two different crimes, two different criminals," said Sadie.

Clarice considered. "Both crimes took place in the False Creek neighbourhood. But you could be right, Number Two, about them being unconnected. We should know better after we've examined the Crime Scenes."

"I'm not too sure about that snooty Priscilla Charles," said Sadie. "I bet she doesn't have a mountain bike. She didn't even know what colour it was!"

"Then why would she say it was stolen?"

"I don't know. But there's something fishy about her." Sadie went back to her book.

Clarice paced about restlessly. "Number Three is usually late, but not this late." She shrugged. "Let's wait another five minutes. If he's not here by then we'll leave him a note explaining we've gone to the Creek to search for clues at the two Crime Scenes. They should be examined while they're still fairly fresh."

After fifteen minutes Brick still had not shown up, so the two girls headed out on their bicycles, splashing through the puddles to False Creek.

They found nothing at The Castings except a couple of candy wrappers and a Skytrain ticket. The mess of muddy footprints on Priscilla Charles' porch made clue-gathering a dirty duty.

Priscilla popped her head out the door just as they were about to leave. "It's the clever detectives," she said brightly. "Have you come to ask more tiresome questions?"

The colour of Clarice's face threatened to

match that of her hair.

"We're searching for clues," explained Sadie quickly.

"Have fun." Priscilla slammed the door.

Wendy Wakabayashi's front garden yielded only a rain-soaked Safeway flyer and a popsicle stick. Clarice studied the roofed crèche of the Holy Family. "Wendy's doll would have been lying here in the straw, I guess."

Sadie pointed. "I see a piece of paper sticking out from under the Baby Jesus."

Clarice leaned over and extracted a candy wrapper. She smoothed it with her fingers. "Robin Hood Milk Chocolate," she read. She handed the wrapper to Sadie. Sadie recorded the find, then pushed it into her pocket.

"Let's pick up some pizza from Granville Market," said Clarice, "and take it back with us for lunch."

They pedalled through Granville Island, past Isadora's Restaurant, past Kids Only Market, under the black shadow of Granville Bridge, through the boardwalk, around the corner at Cottage Books, and up to the bicycle rack at the entrance to the market, where they parked while they picked up their pizza.

When they got back to headquarters there was still no sign of Brick. Sadie's scribbled note lay untouched on the desk.

They ate their pizza.

"I'll keep the clues in this geranium pot for now," said Sadie emptying her pockets of the scraps of paper and the popsicle stick and placing the pot back up on its shelf. She sat down, pulled out her *Tales of Merrie England* and began to read.

Clarice sat and pondered over Sadie's notebook. "It probably means nothing, but both Crime Scenes had Robin Hood chocolate-bar wrappers."

"Hmmnn?" said Sadie absently. She looked up from her book.

"Both Wendy Wakabayashi's and Priscilla Charles' had Robin Hood wrappers," Clarice repeated.

Sadie put her book down. But she wasn't interested in chocolate wrappers. "Clarice, couldn't I have a chair of my own? Having to jump up for a client is not the sort of thing a detective-secretary should have to do. Especially when the client is a just a kid."

"There's no room for another chair."

"I could sit in your chair. Taking notes is difficult when I don't have a chair and desk to work at."

"And where would I sit when I'm asking the questions?"

"You could pace about thoughtfully. All good detectives do that. And while you're pacing you could fire incisive questions."

"What kind of questions are those?"

"Sharp and penetrating. It's from incision which means — "

"Thanks," said Clarice, "I get the picture. Why do I get the feeling you are trying to trick me into letting you use my chair, Number Two?"

"Who, me?" Sadie's eyes widened innocently behind her glasses. "Would I do that?"

Clarice regarded her friend suspiciously.

Sadie said, "If you pace about thoughtfully, clients will be forced to look up at you. This makes them feel respect and awe. Take that Priscilla Charles as an example. She didn't sit; instead she looked down at us and we were forced to look up to her. Snooty people like Priscilla would be put in their place if you were pacing about thoughtfully and firing incisive questions down at them."

"Wouldn't do any harm to try," agreed Clarice. "OK. Sit in my chair when you take your notes next time."

"There's someone outside." Sadie's ears were alert as usual.

"Anyone home?" came a firm voice.

The door rattled open. A thin stick of a girl

stood staring in at the two detectives. Her hair was light brown with a neat white part through the middle and was combed straight down to her ears. Her black jacket hung open, revealing a green 'Save Our Forests' T-shirt and a piece of rose quartz hanging from a leather thong around her neck. Clarice could see the girl's grey eyes take everything in: the desk, the sacks of potatoes stacked against the wall, the shelves of pots and seed catalogues. "So this is the O'Brien Detective Headquarters." Her slightly tilted smile gave her face a kind of "I guessed as much" look.

"Come in and sit down. I'm Clarice O'Brien, Chief Detective, and this is my secretary, Number Two."

"Sadie," said Sadie. "Deputy-Chief Detective."

"I'm Rebecca Wood. Somebody stole my Rollerblades. Do you think you can get them back for me?"

"We could try," said Clarice. She got up and started pacing about thoughtfully. Sadie slid into Clarice's chair and opened her notebook.

"Take a seat," said Clarice.

Rebecca, still smiling, sat in the client chair, reaching into her pocket and pulling out a bar of chocolate. She started to remove the wrapper, changed her mind suddenly, and pushed the bar back into her pocket.

Clarice and Sadie stared at her.

Rebecca saw them staring and pulled out the chocolate from her pocket again. "Like a piece?" She held out the bar to Sadie.

"No thanks," said Sadie. "I'm trying to quit. That stuff is loaded with cholesterol."

She offered some to Clarice who shook her head. "Do you always buy Robin Hood bars?"

"Sometimes." The girl shrugged.

"Full name?" said Clarice. The floor space of the garden shed was so small that Clarice could take only two steps before she had to turn.

"Told you already. Rebecca Wood."

"Where do you live?"

"Here, in Fairview."

"When were your Rollerblades stolen?"

"This morning, about nine o'clock."

"From?"

"My backyard."

"Size and colour?"

Rebecca grinned her tilted grin. "They're black and fluorescent green, size six."

"You usually keep them in your backyard?"

"No. I left them outside for a few minutes while I went in for a glass of milk. When I came back out they were gone."

"Where outside?"

"On the back porch."

"Describe the condition of your Rollerblades when you left them on the porch."

"What do you mean?"

"New, old, clean, dirty, smooth, scuffed. Any distinguishing marks?"

Rebecca frowned. "No. They were in perfect condition. They're brand new — I've only had them for two days. They're an advance gift from my aunt, who's in Hawaii for Christmas."

"Did you see anybody?"

"No."

"How long had you been 'blading before you went in for your glass of milk?"

"I dunno. About an hour maybe."

"Where?"

"On the sea wall, down at the Creek."

Clarice stopped her pacing and studied the girl for a few moments. The she folded her arms and looked directly into the girl's grey eyes. "I want to ask you a very incisive question. How old are you, Rebecca?"

"Eight." Tilted smile.

"Are you sure?"

"Of course I'm sure. I was eight in June."

"That's eight-and-a-half. You seem older."

"I've had a real hard life."

"What is the value of the Rollerblades?"

"Do you mean how much did they cost?"

Clarice nodded, and resumed her pacing. She was taking smaller steps now and was able to take three before having to turn.

"I dunno. I didn't buy them. But they go for about three hundred dollars or so." She smiled easily.

"Seems like the loss of your Rollerblades hasn't upset you too much."

"Sure I'm upset. But I try not to worry about things." She fingered the crystal around her neck.

Clarice stopped her pacing. "That's all for now. Give your address to Number Two. Don't leave town without telling me. We'll be over to check the Scene of the Crime later."

Rebecca stood up.

"If we find your skates the fee is ten dollars plus expenses," said Clarice.

As the door closed on Rebecca Wood's back, Clarice swivelled around to Sadie. "How was that?"

"The best I ever heard you do."

"How was the thoughtful pacing?"

"I was impressed."

"What about the incisive questions?"

"Gave me the shivers all over. I've still got

goosebumps on my arms."

Clarice looked at her friend closely for signs of sarcasm, but Sadie's eyes behind their glasses were as innocent as a doll's.

Chapter 4

No sooner had Rebecca Wood gone than a little boy marched into the office to report the loss of his starship, and for the next hour a steady stream of robbery victims came and went. The O'Brien Detective Agency had never had so many clients. Between visits Clarice managed to hurry into the house and telephone Brick's number, but there was no reply.

"I'm worn out," she said. "Asking all those Incisive Questions and pacing thoughtfully up and down is hard work."

"You do it so well, Clarice."

"Thanks, Number Two. I must say your suggestion was a good one." Her pencil tapped her lip. "Those chocolate wrappers we found at Wendy Wakabayashi's and Priscilla Charles' were Robin Hoods, right?"

Sadie checked her notebook. "That's right. Why?"

"It's just a coincidence, I expect, but Rebecca Wood's bar was a Robin Hood, too."

Sadie dove under the desk and came up holding a Robin Hood wrapper. "I just remembered. This is the one Priscilla Charles threw on the floor." She handed it to Clarice.

Clarice examined the yellow wrapper with its Robin Hood silhouette in milk-chocolate brown. "Must be good chocolate." Pencil tapping lip, she sat staring thoughtfully at the chocolate wrapper. Then she reached up and speared the wrapper on a nail over the desk. She turned to Sadie. "Our next job is to make a list of all the stolen stuff. Could you get it started while I try Brick's number again?"

She was back almost immediately. "Nobody home."

"He's probably shopping or something," said Sadie. "Help me with this list." As Clarice read from Sadie's notes, Sadie made neat columns of information.

Sadie was a perfectionist. Everything she did she had to get exactly right or she wasn't satisfied. Clarice studied the list. "Perfect! Good work, Sadie."

"Thanks."

Clarice made as if to sit in her seat at the desk, but Sadie didn't move. "Could I please have my chair back now?"

"I haven't quite finished checking over my list to make sure everything is right," said Sadie.

"You could do it in the client chair."

Sadie, seeming not to hear Clarice's suggestion, bent over her list checking the names and addresses with the ones in her notebook.

"Sadie! I want my chair back. Now."

Sadie looked up from her list. "Hey! I think I hear Number Three."

But it wasn't Brick. It was a large, red-faced woman wearing a cabbage-green buckskin dress and moccasins. The dress, larger even than its wearer, had long fringes on its sleeves and shoulders, and in several rows from its hemline all the way up to where her chins began. The fringes swung about so wildly as the woman advanced that they made Sadie think of a carwash. The woman came jiggling crazily into the small shed and swooped onto Clarice.

"Clarice, dear," she exclaimed, "give your aunt a hug."

Clarice disappeared inside her huge shivering bulk. When she emerged from the human carwash her face was red and damp and scowling.

"I'm Sadie Stewart," gulped Sadie, jumping

out of Clarice's chair and backing away from the carwash nervously.

"How do you do? I'm Clarice's favourite aunt. You may call me Aunt Esther."

She turned back to her niece, her fringes swinging wildly. "Your dear Uncle Samuel is here in the city for tests." She turned to Sadie. "We're from Horsefly. Samuel hasn't been well since the summer. He must stay in hospital over Christmas."

Her eyes filled with tears. "Tests," she said again. She produced a handkerchief the size of a table napkin from some secret place inside the jungle of green fringes and blew her nose with a loud rasping hoot. "Clarice, dear, I've brought Moonflower out to play with you."

"Where is she?" Sadie craned her neck around Aunt Esther's barrel shape.

Moonflower, appearing as if on cue, emerged from the folds and fringes of her mother's flowing green dress where she had been standing all along. She was wearing a green jacket that came down to her knees.

Clarice and Sadie stared at this sudden apparition. Moonflower suited her name. She was small and slight like a flower, and her eager, upturned face shone like the moon.

"Be kind to each other, children," sobbed

Aunt Esther as she swept out the door, fringes flailing.

"I told you she was loopy," Clarice whispered to Sadie. To her cousin she said, "Too bad about Uncle Samuel, but he'll be OK, don't worry. Sadie and I are kinda busy, so if you don't mind, try to stay out of the way." She pointed to a place in the corner.

Moonflower sat obediently on an upturned clay pot. She was so tiny she fitted neatly into the narrow space between the desk and the lawnmower.

Sadie said, "Your dad's sick. That's tough."

Moonflower nodded. The shine went out of her face.

"So you're Native Indian?" said Sadie. "First Nations?"

Moonflower shook her head regretfully. "Only half."

"Half is better than none," said Sadie, smiling.

"I know," said Moonflower. Her face glowed again.

"I'm really worried about Number Three." Clarice peered out the tiny window in the door.

"Maybe he's been sent back to his home planet," said Sadie.

Moonflower said, "Who is Number Three?"

Clarice went back to studying Sadie's list.

STOLEN ARTICLE	OWNER	PLACE
1. Cabbage Patch doll	Wendy Wakabayashi	85 Foundry Quay, False Creek
2. Mountain bike	Priscilla Charles	648 The Castings, False Creek
3. Rollerblades	Rebecca Wood	2323 Spruce, Fairview
4. Starship	Spider Kennedy	1147 Ferry Row, False Creek
5. Teddy bear	Dana Shannon	17 Millyard, False Creek
6. Raggedy Ann doll	Angie Brown	429 Market Hill, False Creek
7. Tricycle	Melanie Sunderford	778 Lamey's Mill, False Creek

	Item	Name	Address
8.	Fire truck	Connie Chu	11 Alder Walk, False Creek
9.	Walkie-talkie	Aaron Pratt	755 Shoreline, False Creek
10.	Sony Walkman	Julie Clayton	607 Scantlings, False Creek
11.	Portable stereo	Cynthia Tomlin	14 Island Pk. Wk., False Creek
12.	Tricycle	Kim Suzuki	47 Schoolgreen, False Creek
13.	Dump truck	Joey Small	64 Greenchain, False Creek
14.	Tractor	Rocky Furlong	471 Sawcut, False Creek
15.	Radio	Jesse Gallop	580 Scantlings, False Creek

"Number Three is Brick," explained Sadie. "His real name is Leopold Chumley-Smythe. He's a member of our Detective Agency. I'm Number Two, which means second in command — Deputy-Chief — and Clarice is Number One, Chief Detective."

"Sounds like fun," said Moonflower. "Can I be Number Four?" she asked Clarice.

"No, you can't," said Clarice.

"I promise I won't be any trouble."

"Sorry, but no."

Moonflower's face dimmed. She turned to Sadie. "What planet is Number Three from?"

"I was just kidding. He only behaves like an alien. He's almost human really."

"He sounds like fun."

"Oh, he is," said Sadie. "More fun than flossing."

"This is a Crime Wave," muttered Clarice, who was still studying the list. "There's everything from dolls to dump trucks and Rollerblades to radios."

"A toy thief," agreed Sadie. She yawned and pulled her book from her jacket pocket. She started to read.

Clarice paced, the list in her hand.

"I like horses better than toys," said Moonflower.

"Why?" said Clarice.

"Because my Daddy breeds horses. And because I love horses, that's why."

But Clarice's question had not been directed at Moonflower. "Why?" she said again. "Why would anyone steal so much equipment and toys?"

"Beats me," said Sadie.

"Beats me," said Moonflower.

"Don't forget, Clarice," Sadie said, without looking up from her book, "we're still not sure it's only one thief."

"As far as I can see," said Clarice, "only one thing stands out from this list."

"What's that?" asked Sadie.

"All the Crimes were committed in the False Creek neighbourhood except for one. And that one is here in Fairview."

"I hear a bike coming along the back lane," said Sadie.

Clarice rushed to the door. "It's Number Three!"

Brick usually arrived in a spectacular swoop on his bicycle, down the back lane and through the ever-open gate, ending in a startling acrobatic dismount at the garden shed, the Agency headquarters. This afternoon, however, he rode his bicycle like any other boy, and one who has something serious on his mind. His dismount was worse than unspectacular, it was downright awkward.

The door opened slowly. Brick shuffled in, head down, thin shoulders slumped. No high graceful leap through the air, no excited cry, no whirling arms and feet, just a sad and melancholy Brick. He stood, hands lifeless at his sides, staring gloomily at Clarice. "Sorry I'm late, Chief."

"This is Moonflower," said Sadie.

Brick noticed the tiny girl in the corner. "Hi," he said morosely.

Moonflower got up and shook his lifeless hand. "My grandfather is a Chief," she said solemnly. She stood back and studied his spiky yellow head. "I like your hair."

"Thanks," Brick said automatically. "Yours is fine, too," he added to be polite.

Moonflower's hair was straight and long and dark. She smiled at Brick. "And I like your eyes. I never saw yellow eyes before."

But Brick's eyes had lost their usual glow, and Moonflower's compliments failed to restore it. He turned and pulled himself laboriously up onto the potato sacks and sat staring at the knees of his tattered jeans.

All this time Clarice had said nothing; instead she had been studying Brick, searching for the reason for his sorrow. Now she said, "What's the problem, Number Three?"

Brick kicked his heels at the sacks. "Bad news."

"What is it?" said Sadie. "Maybe we can help."

"They're sending him back to Africa."

"Who?" asked Sadie.

"My father."

"Who's sending him?" Sadie pursued doggedly.

"His company."

"Your father's company is sending him back to Africa," said Sadie.

Brick nodded gloomily.

Clarice and Sadie digested this information.

"I knew there was something wrong," said Clarice. "My Sixth Sense told me. I had a Hunch."

"After Christmas," said Brick mournfully.

"So you and your mom have to go, too."

Brick nodded.

Moonflower said, "Africa?"

"That's where he's from," explained Sadie. "He was brought up by lions in the jungle."

"Really?" said Moonflower.

"That's what he says," said Sadie. "Myself, I think it was monkeys." Then she pushed at her glasses in embarrassment. "Only kidding,

Number Three."

"You don't want to go back?" asked Moon-flower.

Brick shook his head.

"Any chance they'll change their minds?" said Clarice.

Brick shook his head again.

A silence dark and deep fell on the little garden shed, and suddenly the air felt cold. Moonflower pulled her jacket down around her knees; Sadie hunched her shoulders; Clarice rubbed her hands together briskly.

When he saw how sad everyone was, Brick seemed to brighten up a little. "Anything new, Chief?"

Clarice handed him Sadie's list. "It's a Big Case. Toys of all kinds." She paused. "Looks like this will be your last case, Number Three. I don't know how we'll be able to carry on without you." While Brick examined the list the three girls looked at one another in worried silence.

Even Sadie had nothing to say.

Chapter 5

Clarice broke the silence at last. "No good standing around like a flock of Canada geese. Let's get out there and examine the Scenes of the Crimes. We've got to find some Clues if we're ever going break this Case." Clarice might be sad, but nothing could keep her from speaking in capitals when she was at work.

They headed toward the Creek. Clarice led the way, striding purposefully. Moonflower slipped her hand into Sadie's as they followed. Brick trailed slowly behind.

The first crime scene was Alder Walk. They made their way along the waterfront under the shadows of the three great bridges that linked the inlet to the downtown office towers. Behind the towers the white-capped North Shore mountains rose to the clouds.

They knocked on the door of the townhouse and got permission to search around the flower boxes and the garden area in the front where Connie Chu had left her firetruck.

"If you see any candy wrappers," instructed Clarice, "don't touch them, call me."

"There's one over here, Clarice," said Moonflower, "on the porch. It's sticking out from underneath a carton of Coke bottles."

Clarice bent and examined the wrapper without touching it. "A Robin Hood bar. Just as I figured." She pulled it out from under the carton and handed it to Sadie.

"What does it mean?" said Sadie.

"We'll see," said Clarice mysteriously. "My Hunch is there'll be one at each Crime Scene. Look for it."

Clarice was right. At each crime scene they found a Robin Hood chocolate wrapper wedged under some object like a boot or a rock or a leg of a garden chair or table.

After they had trudged through what seemed like a hundred rain-soaked yards, Clarice said, "Well, that's that! Let's quit."

Sadie consulted her list. "There's still two to do. Fairview — Rebecca Wood's Rollerblades — and we haven't done Greenchain here in the Creek."

Clarice said, "OK, we'll finish the Creek with Greenchain. Fairview can wait until tomorrow. Where is Greenchain?"

Sadie said, "I dunno. Number Three?"

Brick shrugged his thin shoulders.

"Probably one of those short, cobbled streets up near Bucketwheel," said Sadie. "We should have brought a map."

"This is your neighbourhood, Number Two," said Clarice impatiently. "I didn't think we'd need a map."

"We could ask someone," suggested Sadie.

"There it is," said Moonflower, pointing off across the Charleson picnic grounds. "It's over there."

"How do you know?" said Sadie.

"I can see the street sign."

The others looked. "I don't see a sign," said Sadie.

"Me neither," said Clarice. "Number Three, you see a sign?"

"No, Chief."

Moonflower said, "Come on, I'll show you." She led the way across the wet grass, and five minutes later they were at Greenchain. Moonflower pointed to the sign. "See? It says Greenchain."

The others were speechless.

Clarice was the first to find her voice. "But how could you see that sign from ..." She waved her arms helplessly.

"From at least half a kilometre away!" said an unbelieving Sadie.

Moonflower said, "I've got eagle eyes. Runs in my family."

"Eagle eyes?" said Sadie edging closer to Clarice's little cousin to inspect her big dark eyes.

"My grandfather's name is Soars With Eagles." Moonflower began to speak in a singsong voice. "Even though he's very old he can see, from great distances, a speeding sparrow hawk or a spider spinning a delicate web. He can see the mice in the fields and the footprints of the Great Spirit who walks in the forest."

Brick, who had climbed the Greenchain sign and was chinning himself rather half-heartedly on the arm of the post, missed most of Moonflower's speech, but the two girls stared at her in astonishment.

Moonflower said, "Those are my father's words. I learned them, and they're true."

"Let's go," said Clarice taking her little cousin proudly by the hand.

"Thought you said your cousin would be a nuisance," whispered Sadie to Clarice as they made their way along the cobbled street.

Greenchain was paved in puddles; raindrops hung glistening like jewels in the cedar hedges.

"Keep your eyes open for Clues," said Clarice as they approached Joey Small's townhouse.

Sadie glanced into her plastic Safeway bag. "Except for the Robin Hood wrappers, we haven't found much so far. A squashed Big Mac box, a few bird feathers, an empty Coke bottle, an Oreo cookie bag, and a smashed cassette of the Mormon Tabernacle Choir singing 'Best Loved Christmas Carols'."

"Could be Valuable Clues," said Clarice.

"I love Christmas carols," said Moonflower.

"The robber probably came through here," said Clarice pointing to a gap in the hedge. "Come on." She led the way through the gap. "Search thoroughly."

The Robin Hood wrapper was speared onto the bare branch of a small tree. Moonflower was the first to spot it. Sadie made a note and added it to their collection. There was nothing else, only a feather on the wet grass.

"Canada goose feather," said Sadie.

"How do you know it's a Canada goose?" said Clarice.

"It's the right colour, brown with white near the quill," said Sadie. She felt a comment coming on, and try as hard as she could, she wasn't able to keep it from tumbling out. "And I know it's a goose because of its size. You don't see too many sparrows and starlings with feathers a foot long."

Clarice didn't seem to notice the sarcasm. "Could be a Valuable Clue."

"Oh, sure," said Sadie, who was cold and tired. "The toys were all stolen by a flock of Canada geese! It's obvious when you think about it for a minute. I wish I had your powerful sixth sense, Clarice, I really do!"

The idea of geese stealing toys made Moonflower giggle.

Clarice said, "Write in your notebook, 'one candy wrapper and one feather'." Sadie, recognizing the stiffness in her friend's voice, knew she had gone too far. Clarice glared at her. "Moonflower thinks you're hilarious, Number Two."

A large black-and-white hound rushed through the gap in the hedge. It growled at them and showed its teeth.

"Look out!" yelled Clarice.

Moonflower ducked behind Clarice, her eyes wide with fright. Sadie rushed and hid behind Brick.

"Hrrr gkklgg," Brick said quietly to the dog.

The dog stopped growling and regarded Brick with polite interest. Brick said, "Hrrr gkklgg" again, and then, "Mmmnggkkkll." The dog wagged its tail and grinned.

Brick knelt down in the wet grass. He stroked the dog's ruff and murmured quietly into its ear. The dog nuzzled Brick's hand. "Wuff," said the dog.

Moonflower came out from behind Clarice and stroked the dog's wet coat. "He understands you," she said to Brick.

Sadie said, "He talks to cats and lobsters. Worms and spiders too, I bet." She shivered at the thought of it.

"It's because he was raised by lions," explained Clarice.

"What is the dog saying?" asked Moonflower.

Brick frowned. "Just dog stuff." He shrugged. "Dogs don't know very much. But they tell you everything they know, not like cats."

"What do cats say?" said Moonflower.

Brick ran a hand through the dog's coat as he turned to Moonflower. "Cats? They know almost everything, but they say nothing."

"Horses know a lot," said Moonflower eagerly. "As much as cats I betcha. Can you talk to horses too, Brick? I love horses. Would you teach me to talk to horses?"

Brick smiled but said nothing.

By now the dog was lying on his back letting Moonflower scratch his belly. A ginger cat poked her head through the gap in the hedge to see what all the fuss was about. The dog gave a yelp and leaped up. Then, barking madly, he took off after the cat and disappeared through the hedge.

"Goodbye, dog," said Moonflower.

"That cat looked familiar," said Sadie.

"Ginger," said Brick.

"What you kids doin' over there?" came a woman's voice from over the fence.

Sadie groaned.

"Oh, no, it's Dolly Varden!" said Clarice.

Dolly Varden and her cat, Ginger, had caused the three detectives much embarrassment and irritation on a previous case. Now here she was again, a large woman with a large voice.

She stood glaring at them, her thick arms folded across her ample chest and her double chin wobbling in indignation. "Well, I never!" she exclaimed. "Herbert!" she called into the house. "Call the police! It's them kids tryin' to steal Ginger again!"

Herbert, a small man with a big moustache, poked his bald head out the door. He looked like a walrus. "Right ho, Dolly!" He disappeared inside.

"Come on," said Clarice, "let's go!" She grasped Moonflower's hand, and they all scrambled out the gap in the hedge. They ran away down the street, and didn't stop running until the danger was far behind.

"Phew! That woman ought to be put away," puffed Sadie.

"Never mind," said Clarice. "We finished our examinations of the Crime Scenes, most of them anyway. We can finish up tomorrow. And we know now that all the Crimes have one thing in common — Robin Hood chocolate wrappers."

When they got back to headquarters, Brick slid onto his bicycle and made toward home.

"See you tomorrow, Number Three," called Clarice.

" 'Bye, Brick," said Moonflower.

Brick waved without looking back.

Sadie was next. She mounted her bicycle and shoved off. "I left the bag of clues on the desk, Clarice." Her long hair streamed behind her as Clarice and Moonflower waved goodbye and watched her disappear into the December gloom.

Chapter 6

The next morning, Sadie rode her bicycle up to the Agency office, carefully avoiding the muddy puddles. "I'm dreaming of a white Christmas," she sang.

Clarice, wearing a yellow tuque against the suddenly cold weather, was in her backyard pumping up the tires of a child's bicycle. "What's to sing about?"

"No rain, no pain," said Sadie. She propped her bicycle against the end of the shed, then stood and watched Clarice pumping. "You sound like you lost your favourite grandmother, Clarice."

"I've been thinking about Number Three. I'll really miss him."

"Maybe he won't go. They might change their minds."

"People have to go wherever their work takes them."

"Maybe they'll go but leave him behind. If I were his parents I'd seriously consider running away from home."

"Does that New Year's resolution of yours include being nicer to people?"

"You're right, Clarice. I'm sorry." Sadie looked around. "Where is he anyway? Late as usual, I suppose."

Clarice paused for breath. "If you feel a sudden uncontrollable urge to help instead of just standing there, you could haul your hands from your pockets and check the tires of my bike for me."

Sadie glanced at Clarice's bicycle leaning against the recycling bins at the back gate, but made no move to help. She nodded at the bike Clarice was working on.

"That bike for Moonflower?" she asked.

"That's right."

Sadie leaned down to peer more closely at the dusty bicycle. "Joanne Fox had one of these Hubbles, remember? Chain had a nasty habit of jumping off when she was freewheeling down the Slopes. Something wrong with the brakes too; the brake blocks kept flying out like bullets from a gun whenever the wheels were spinning fast. Very dangerous. Joanne's dad finally pitched the bike in the garbage after poor Joanne fell off and broke her clavicle."

Clarice pumped and puffed.

"Clavicle is the scientific word for collar bone."

Clarice pumped faster.

"You sure you want little Moonflower to ride this old thing?"

Clarice connected the pump to the rear wheel of the Hubble and continued her vigorous pumping.

"She could have my Horwood Dart. The one I got when I was six, remember? It's still like new."

Clarice uncoupled the pump. Her face was very red, and only some of it was from the exertion of pumping. She opened her mouth to say something, but Sadie had already gone into the garden shed.

Clarice tested the Hubble by pushing it along and testing the brakes. She did this until her temper had cooled, and then she leaned the bicycle against the shed and followed Sadie in.

Sadie shivered. "We could use a heater in here."

"Help me spread the Clues out on the desk and make a proper list," said Clarice. "That should help warm you up. We'll need your notebook."

The two girls leaned over the desk sorting and arranging candy wrappers, bird feathers, potato-chip bags, styrofoam cups and boxes, plastic picnic forks, and miscellaneous bits and pieces into crime-scene groups. Then Sadie sat down to make a list in her neat handwriting while Clarice called out detailed descriptions and locations.

"What do you make of the Robin Hood wrappers at each crime scene?" asked Sadie.

"I'm still thinking about it," said Clarice.

When they were finished, Clarice glanced through the list. "Good work, Number Two. We can study it later. Right now I've got a Plan." She pulled her tuque down more firmly over her red head. "Let's go."

"But where's Moonflower?"

"Out shopping in the mall with her mom. And then they go visit Uncle Samuel at the hospital."

"And what about Number Three?" Sadie scrambled after her.

Clarice stopped and thought. "We could stop at his place on the way." She led the way out the door.

"Don't forget the crime scene on Spruce we're supposed to visit this morning — the girl who lost her Rollerblades, remember? Rebecca Wood."

"I already biked over there this morning before you got here."

"What did you find?"

"Nothing," said Clarice. "There was nothing there."

"What do you mean, there was nothing there?" asked Sadie. "We've found a Robin Hood wrapper at every scene so far. Why would Rebecca Wood's place be any different from the others?"

"There was nothing there," said Clarice, "because there is no 2300 block on Spruce Street. There's a 2200 block and there's a 2400 block, but what should be the 2300 block is Choklit Park. No houses. Just bushes and grass."

"No houses!" said Sadie. "But there must be houses! Rebecca lives at 2323 Spruce Street."

"You must have copied down the wrong address," said Clarice.

"I did no such thing. If my notebook says 2323 Spruce, then 2323 Spruce it is."

"You made an error, Number Two."

Sadie did not like being accused of making a mistake. "Look here, Clarice — " she began angrily.

"Chief," said Clarice loftily. "You should call me Chief. We're on a Case and when we're on a Case I'm Chief Detective and you're Number Two."

"I'm sick of being called Number Two. I'm a person, not a computer, Clarice. I'm a living, breathing person."

"And living, breathing people make mistakes, Number Two. Maybe you thought the girl said 2323 Spruce when she was probably saying 3323 or maybe 4323."

"Clarice, my ears are never wrong. I've got Superior Hearing, remember?"

Clarice shrugged, and mounted her bicycle. Sadie pushed off behind her and a few minutes later they were at Brick's townhouse. They dismounted and leaned their bicycles against the wall.

Clarice rang the doorbell. They waited.

"Nobody home," said Clarice.

"I can hear someone vacuuming upstairs," said Sadie. She held her finger on the bell.

Clarice said, "That's enough." They waited.

"You ever been in Number Three's place before, Clarice?"

Clarice shook her head. "Never."

"Wonder what it's like?" said Sadie.

The door opened. It was Brick's mother. They had met her before. She had spiky yellow hair, just like her son's. "Hello, Mrs. Chumley-Smythe," said Clarice.

Brick's mother smiled. "Hello, girls. You've

come for Leopold? I saw his bicycle in the back, so he's probably in his room." She yelled down the stairs. "Leopold!"

There was no answer.

Mrs. Chumley-Smith opened the door wider. "Why don't you go down."

The two girls stepped inside and started down the stairs to the basement. Brick's mother went back to her vacuuming.

The basement was unfinished. They edged past the hot water tank and the washer and dryer and found themselves at an unfinished mahogany door.

Clarice knocked.

Silence.

"Number Three!" called Clarice.

"He's not there," said Sadie.

Clarice turned the handle, pushed the door open, and looked in.

All was dark. They could see nothing. Clarice fumbled around the door frame and found the light switch. The one window in the room had been blinded by a heavy, dark curtain. Brick was not there.

The girls stared. Except for a circular straw mat in the middle of the floor, the room was almost bare. There were no books, no clothing strewn about, no furniture of any kind. One of the wood-panelled walls was scored with a thousand scratches. The room had a strange musky smell.

The girls looked at each other in astonishment. Sadie's mouth moved but no sounds came out. Clarice closed the door carefully.

"Let's go," she said.

They said goodbye to Brick's mother and five minutes later were pedalling slowly, thoughtfully, silently, toward False Creek.

After a while, Clarice stopped. Sadie pulled up behind her.

"My Hunch," said Clarice, "is that Number Three sleeps on that straw mat."

Sadie nodded. "If he was really brought up by lions, then I guess it figures." She didn't sound too certain.

"Why do you think he keeps his room so dark?"

Sadie shrugged. "Maybe it seems more like a den that way." She frowned. "What did you make of all those scratches on the wall?"

Clarice shook her head.

"Clarice, you don't suppose those scratches are . . ."

"Santa Claws? Come on," said Clarice, mounting her bicycle."We gotta concentrate on our Case." She pushed off.

"Wait up, Clarice, what's all the rush? Where are we going?"

"My Plan, remember? We're going fishing for the criminal. But first we need bait." She headed her bicycle toward False Creek.

Chapter 7

Sadie pedalled furiously to catch up. "Fishing? Bait? Number Three's place must have got to you. Your brain has crumbled, Clarice. What fishing? What bait?"

"Bait is a toy. We need a doll or a dump truck, something for the bandit to steal."

"I get it," puffed Sadie. "A stake-out. We hide and wait for him to steal it. Then we leap out and catch him, right?"

"Right, we collar the thief. And it might not be a him."

"You think it's a girl?"

"Could be, why not? A Good Detective keeps an Open Mind."

They rode over the Alder Street bridge that connected Fairview to False Creek and were soon in the bandit's territory. A cold wind blew up the water from under the Cambie Bridge and rattled and tinkled the bells on the marina sailboats. The sea wall was busy with walkers and shoppers on their way to and from Granville Market. Christmas music on TVs and radios escaped into the cold air from the townhouses close to the sea wall, mingling with the chorus of sailboat bells.

"Look," said Clarice, "there's a kid with a doll." She pointed over to the other side of Sawyers Lane, where a little girl was playing with her doll on the front steps of her townhouse. The townhouse was decorated with flashing red and green Christmas lights looped in strings underneath the windows and around the doorway.

"Hi, kid," said Clarice, "you need a babysitter?"

The little girl considered. "Babysitter?"

"What's your doll's name?" asked Sadie.

"Sleepy Susan. Her eyes close when she lies down. And she wets. Would you like to see her wet?"

"No," said Clarice. "Thanks all the same."

"And she makes rude noises just like real babies. Would you like to hear her make a rude noise?"

"Some other time maybe," said Clarice. "This

is Sadie and my name is Clarice."

"My name is Amy Martin, and I'm five years old," said the little girl proudly.

Sadie said, "Why don't you go on in and grab a peanut butter sandwich and a glass of milk. We'll babysit Sleepy Susan for you."

"OK," agreed Amy, who seemed to like the idea of babysitting. "I'll put her to bed. Don't wake her up." She wrapped the doll in a pink blanket and placed it on the top of a low wall next to the townhouse steps. Amy kissed her doll, then went inside.

Clarice said, "Come on," and jumped over the low wall. Sadie followed. "Keep down out of sight," said Clarice.

They sat on the cold concrete, a few metres from the sleeping doll. "All we do now," said Clarice, "is wait."

After only a few minutes Amy peeked out to make sure her doll was being babysat properly. "Just checking," she said.

Clarice and Sadie waited for the bandit to fall into their trap.

After half an hour Amy came out again and stood on the top step, peering over the wall. "We're still here," said Clarice. Amy skipped back inside.

"I'm frozen," said Sadie.

They waited.

Sadie said, "If you get frostbite, gangrene sets in and they have to amputate."

Clarice said nothing.

"People lose their fingers and toes. They even lose hands and feet."

Clarice said, "Hush!"

"Their limbs freeze and go black and then they have to be chopped off."

Silence.

"Scott of the Antarctic was a famous explorer and he lost some of his men that way. When a man got frostbitten feet and couldn't walk any more through the intense cold, he crawled out of his sleeping bag at night when the others were asleep. Then he would stagger away into the blizzard, never to be found."

Silence.

"Don't you want to know why he did that?"

"Number Two, please! We have to be quiet."

"Well, he did it as an act of great and noble heroism. He didn't want to hold the others back from making it safely home, so he sacrificed himself."

Clarice said nothing.

"Clarice, your blood is hotter than mine. You don't feel the cold the way I do. This stake-out is extremely heroic of me. I bet my fingers and toes are turning black already."

Clarice said, "Sh-sh-sssh!"

They waited.

Sadie pulled out her Merrie England book and started to read.

Clarice, hands in pockets, shoulders hunched, didn't take her eyes off the doll on the wall.

After a while, Sadie pushed Merrie England back into her jacket pocket. "It's too cold to read. And this concrete is damp from all the rain. My behind feels like a popsicle."

"A Good Detective has to get used to being uncomfortable. Duty Comes Before Comfort," Clarice whispered in capitals.

Sadie was so cold she forgot her New Year's resolution. "Wow! What a great slogan!" she said furiously. "Duty before comfort. Terrific! If my fingers weren't so frozen I would write that down for posterity!"

Clarice gave a sigh.

"Just think," Sadie continued, making no attempt to keep her voice low, "I'll bet hundreds of clever things have been said throughout history, but because nobody wrote them down they're lost for ever. What a waste! But I'll remember, and someday the name of Clarice O'Brien will stand alongside such great names as Shakespeare and Judy Blume. What was it again? Comfort Before Duty? Or was it Duty Before Comfort?"

By the time Sadie got to the end of her long speech, Clarice was furious. "Number Two, will you shut up! All that blabbing! How can we expect to collar the thief if you keep . . ."

"Hush!" said Sadie.

Clarice lunged at Sadie as though about to throttle her. "You tell me to hush! You're the one whose blabbing is ruining my stake-out!"

"Hush, I tell you," said Sadie. "I hear something."

"Huh?" said Clarice. She swivelled around. She leaped to her feet. She made choking sounds. She waved her arms wildly.

Sadie watched her in surprise. "Clarice?"

Clarice pointed. "The doll!" she screamed. "It's gone!"

Chapter 8

Sleepy Susan had disappeared.

Clarice jumped over the wall. Sadie followed. They looked up the lane and down the lane, but not a single body was to be seen: the lane was deserted.

"Stolen!" moaned Clarice. "From right under our noses."

"Where's Sleepy Susan?" It was Amy standing in the doorway, framed by Christmas lights. "What have you done with her?"

"Your doll has been stolen," said Clarice grimly. "But we're Detectives. We'll get her back for you, don't worry."

Amy began to cry. She turned and ran back inside.

"Let's go, Sadie!"

Sadie needed no urging: she was ready for

flight. They leaped onto their bicycles and retreated madly along the sea wall, casting anxious glances back over their shoulders.

When they were a safe distance away Clarice's feisty temper seized her. "We lost him! We could have had him, but we lost him!"

"Well, don't blame me," said Sadie.

"You ruined my Plan with all that blabbing!"

Sadie bristled. "I do my best to provide bright, entertaining conversation on a cold, boring stake-out, and this is the thanks I get!"

Clarice stormed along in silence, her fists clenched tight around her handlebars and her expression grim.

As they crossed the Alder bridge, Sadie, anxious to make amends, called out, "Clarice?"

But Clarice was still furious. By the time they reached Headquarters, however, her anger had gone. Clarice never held grudges. She turned to Sadie. "Come on, it's only three days to Christmas; we've got to catch this criminal. Let's patrol on our bikes until lunchtime. We might spot him."

"We could ask any kids we see if they've seen anyone suspicious," Sadie suggested.

"OK." They pushed off once again. "We're a team, Sadie," said Clarice. "Even if one of us louses up, we're still a team. We just gotta get back in there and pitch."

"Right," agreed Sadie. "You mustn't feel bad you loused up, Clarice. We're a team." Clarice gazed at Sadie for a moment, then shook her head.

They patrolled till lunchtime. After a lunch of bagels and cream cheese at the Granville Island Market they returned to the Agency office. They found two messages in their coffee-can mailbox.

"Two more robberies," said Clarice, handing them to Sadie, "but this time they're here in Fairview."

Sadie scanned the messages. "A doll and a skateboard. I'll add 'em to the crimesheet with Amy Martin's Sleepy Susan."

While she was writing, Brick arrived at last. His bicycle scraped and bounced and rattled sorrowfully. He slouched into the office.

"Two more robberies, Number Three," said Clarice. "We gotta catch this thief and make the neighbourhood safe for kids again."

"Right, Chief." Brick hardly glanced at the two girls. He gave a sigh and climbed dejectedly onto his potato perch.

"Cheer up, Number Three," said Clarice. "We'll miss you very much, but try to look on the bright side. Africa isn't all that bad. You'll get used to it again — all those animals you love:

lions and tigers and elephants." She patted his worn runner. "Why, you could be an animal detective, you know, catching murdering ivory traders."

"That's right," said Sadie, pulling at the lace of his other runner. "You could leap out of the jungle at them. Frighten them to death I should think."

The door opened. Moonflower slipped in quietly and sat in her place in the corner.

Clarice asked cautiously, "Any news of Uncle Samuel?"

Moonflower shook her head sadly.

"I've got a bike for you to ride."

"Thanks, Clarice." Moonflower smiled a small smile.

"How did you enjoy Christmas shopping in the big city?" said Sadie to get Moonflower's thoughts off her father's illness.

Moonflower brightened up. "The mall is wonderful. Santa sits on a throne in the middle of a big Christmas-tree forest, and there's elves in green and dwarfs with funny ears and noses working with hammers and — "

"Hey! Slow down," said Sadie.

" — there's Rudolph and all the reindeers — "

"Moonflower!" said Sadie.

"I talked with Santa."

Clarice said, "That woolly whiskered old fraud."

"What's a fraud?" asked Moonflower.

"A phoney," explained Sadie. "But take no notice of Clarice. She doesn't believe in Santa Claus."

"I know the mall Santa isn't the real one," said Moonflower. "He's only a helper. But I told him about the letter I faxed to the real Santa at the North Pole."

Sadie was surprised. "Santa Claus has a fax number?"

"Of course," said Moonflower.

"I always write a letter," said Sadie. "What did you ask him for?"

"Two very special things," said Moonflower seriously.

"What things?"

"I can't tell. It's a secret between me and Santa."

Brick spoke. "Any luck, Chief?" Clarice was studying the list of clues and tapping her lip with her pencil. She didn't hear him.

Sadie said to Brick, "We almost caught the bandit in a trap. But we let him get away. We didn't even see him."

Tap-tap went Clarice's pencil.

"I'm hungry," said Sadie.

"I've got something," said Clarice.

"Well, hand it over. I could eat a hippopotamus."

"No, I mean I think I've found something."

"Even a stick of gum would help."

"It's about those Robin Hood chocolate wrappers," said Clarice. "So far we've found one at each Crime Scene."

"Except at the Sleepy Susan scene," said Sadie, "and the two new ones we haven't examined yet."

"But they do link the robberies together, agreed?"

"Except for Priscilla Charles," said Sadie. "She drops wrappers all over the place."

"Carelessly dropped ones don't count," said Clarice. "Priscilla and Rebecca had Robin Hood bars — we saw them — but that isn't the same. Think back. The wrappers we found at the Crime Scenes were placed deliberately, wedged or weighted in place so they wouldn't blow away. Why? Because the bandit wanted us to find them. But why? Why does he want us to find them? That's the big question — why?"

"That's easy," said Sadie. "He's a show-off. It's like leaving a sign. It's like he's laughing at us. The Robin Hood wrapper is his calling card, like the mark of Zorro. Zorro always left a big Z carved with the point of his sword."

"You've got it, Number Two!" said Clarice, her freckled face flushed and her blue eyes flashing with excitement. "You've got it! But why Robin Hood? Why not some other wrapper, like O Henry?"

"He likes milk chocolate," Brick suggested.

"No," said Clarice. "I'll tell you why. The bandit leaves Robin Hoods because he *is* Robin Hood. He wants us to know who he is and he wants us to know his Motive!"

"What's motive?" said Moonflower.

"It's the reason for the crime," said Sadie. She frowned. "You mean our bandit is stealing from the rich kids in False Creek to give to the poor kids somewhere else?"

Clarice grinned. "Exactly!"

Sadie said, "I think you're right, Clarice, but that's no hunch."

"What do you mean? Of course it's a Hunch. It's one of my typical Sixth Sense Hunches."

"Call it what you like," said Sadie, "but in my opinion it was brilliant reasoning, not a hunch. I've got Superior Reasoning Powers myself," she admitted modestly, "but even I failed to hit on the meaning of the Robin Hood wrappers."

"Wow!" said Brick looking at Clarice with solemn admiration.

"I should have been the one who thought of

it," said Sadie pulling her Merrie England book from her pocket. "I don't know why I didn't. I've been reading about Robin Hood for three days."

"Who is Robin Hood?" Moonflower asked Brick.

Brick said, "The guy in the movie with the bow and arrows."

"I didn't see the movie," said Moonflower.

Sadie pointed to the picture of Robin Hood on the cover of her book and explained, "He was a famous bandit in England hundreds of years ago before guns were invented. He lived in Sherwood Forest with his band of merry men."

"Why were they merry?" said Moonflower.

"Because they liked living in the forest," said Sadie. "He used a bow and arrows to rob the rich and give to the poor. The poor people loved him."

"Robbed the rich?" said Moonflower. "How?"

"Easy. His merry men just dropped out of the trees on top of the rich people who travelled through the forest on their horses."

"Why were they travelling through the forest?" asked Moonflower.

"It was the only way to get to Nottingham."

"And he gave to the poor people?" said Moonflower.

"That's right."

"Didn't he keep any money for himself and his merry men?"

"He had no use for money," said Sadie. "Everything they needed was in Sherwood Forest."

Moonflower was excited by Sadie's story. "Wasn't it very dangerous, robbing the rich?"

"Robin Hood loved danger."

"Did he hurt the rich people?"

"Never. Only their pockets."

Moonflower laughed with pleasure. "What did he look like?"

"Very handsome, with flashing white teeth. He wore an outfit of Lincoln green, so he couldn't be seen in the great leafy forest, and so did his merry men."

Clarice had been silent all this time, her face flushed, her foot tapping impatiently. Now she said sharply, "If we could get back to the Case?"

"I would never have figured out the motive," said Sadie admiringly. "You're the greatest child detective in the world, Clarice."

"Thank you, Number Two." Clarice nodded graciously. "The Case is a long way from being solved, but there's an important lesson here. To solve a Case a Good Detective must understand Motive, and if she understands Motive, then she begins to understand the Criminal Mind."

"Great stuff, Chief!" said Brick.

Encouraged by Brick and Sadie's admiration, Clarice began to lecture. "Our criminal obviously thinks of himself as a modern-day Robin Hood. He steals from the rich to give to the poor. He is overconfident, so he leaves his calling card in the form of a chocolate-bar wrapper with a clue to his identity, thinking he can't be caught and not realizing we will discover his Motive."

"As a challenge!" agreed Sadie. "Like a knight of old throwing down his gauntlet."

"Yes. A challenge," said Clarice.

"It's like saying, 'Catch me if you can'," said Sadie.

"This is so exciting," said Moonflower. "Lincoln green will be my favourite colour from now on. Is my jacket Lincoln green, do you think?"

Sadie pounced. "That's it! Green! I bet he wears green like the real Robin Hood!"

"If he's wearing green then he should be easy to spot," said Clarice. "Good work, Number Two. I think you're right. It fits in with the workings of the Criminal Mind. All we need do is look for someone dressed in green and follow him."

"Wow!" said Brick again.

"It was nothing," said Sadie modestly.

"Thank you," said Clarice, at the same time.

"Lincoln green," said Moonflower, stroking

her jacket.

"It gets dark early," said Clarice, "so let's move out. We should examine the two new Crime Scenes, but first let's check back at Amy's Sleepy Susan Scene for a chocolate wrapper."

"Clarice, we really will be world-famous detectives one day," said Sadie. "I'm sure of it!"

Chapter 9

Before they set out, Moonflower tested the little bicycle around Clarice's backyard. The others watched her. She jumped off, happy, her face flushed. "It's just right, Clarice!"

"Then let's go," said Clarice.

They found the chocolate wrapper on the wall directly over the spot where they had been hiding in their stake-out. It was anchored in place by a small rock. "Another calling card," said Clarice.

"Right over our heads!" said Sadie in wonderment. "And we didn't know it!"

"He made fools of us," said Clarice. "He's slippery and he's smart."

"Like Robin Hood," said Moonflower.

"Take a look at this," said Sadie, her glasses only a few centimetres away from the top of the rough-textured wall.

They all looked. "Bits of fluff," said Clarice.

"Cloth fibres," said Sadie. "Fleece or wool."

"Let me see," said Moonflower, who was too small to reach. Clarice lifted her. "Lincoln green," said Moonflower.

"Well, it's green all right," said Sadie. "Must have rubbed off the arm of his jacket while he was fixing his calling card in place."

"You've found a Very Important Clue, Number Two," said Clarice. "It means that the thief probably does wear green. Good work!"

Sadie blushed with pleasure.

"So keep your eyes open for anyone wearing a green outfit," said Clarice. "In the meantime we've got to come up with a Plan."

"Not another stake-out," pleaded Sadie, "it's too cold."

"No more stake-outs," agreed Clarice. "That green bandit is too smart to be trapped that easily."

"Just like the real Robin," said Moonflower.

"That's right," said Sadie. "The Sheriff of Nottingham couldn't trap him. He was too smart. Besides, when Robin was in the forest nobody could see him because of his green outfit. He was invisible."

"That's where our Robin is making his big

mistake," said Clarice.

"What do you mean?" said Moonflower.

"If he's wearing green," Sadie explained, "we'll see him. There's no forest to hide him."

"He'll stand out like a walking Christmas tree," said Clarice.

"What's the next move, Chief?" said Brick who, bored with all the talk, was trying to ride his bicycle along the narrow wall.

"Your next move will be to the funeral home if you fall off that wall," said Sadie.

Brick ignored her.

"We gotta go back to Fairview and interview the two new victims," said Clarice. "And after that it's brainstorming time."

An hour later they were finished and had added two more Robin Hood calling cards to their collection. It was now beginning to get dark and the tired detectives were about ready to call it a day. Suddenly Clarice shouted "Look! It's him! It's Robin Hood!"

The others looked. A burly teenaged boy in a green sweatsuit was running down the hill, heading for the Alder bridge to False Creek.

"He's just a jogger," said Sadie.

"But he could be the thief," said Clarice excitedly. "He's wearing a green suit. And he's carrying something. Probably just stole it!"

Moonflower narrowed her eyes. "Sony Walkman," she said reading the name on the teenager's tape player. "He's wearing earphones."

"Lots of joggers have them," said Sadie.

But Clarice was not convinced. "Best to make sure. After him!" she cried, leading the way.

The others pedalled after her. Brick passed her easily. "Stop him, Number Three," Clarice yelled.

"OK, Chief," answered Brick, glad to have something interesting to do. He soon caught up to the teenager, and rode easily along beside him. "The Chief wants to talk to you," he yelled into his earphone.

The boy looked over his shoulder and saw three children pedalling furiously after him. "Get lost, kid," he snarled at Brick, "can't you see I'm busy?" Brick flicked his foot casually at the boy's ankle. The green-suited figure tumbled to the ground and started to yell.

"Good work, Number Three," puffed Clarice.

The teenager scrambled to his feet. His face was purple. He clenched a fist and glared at Brick. "I'm angry!" he yelled. "I'm very angry!" He snatched off his earphones.

"Hold it right there," yelled Clarice.

"You are about to be snapped like a twig!" the boy yelled at Brick.

Brick stood casually beside his bicycle. "I asked him nicely, Chief, but he wouldn't stop."

"That's all right, Number Three. I'll take over now." To the fuming teenager she said, "I'm Clarice O'Brien investigating a Case of Stolen Property." She flashed her ID. "I have reason to believe that you are Robin Hood."

The boy stared. "Robin — " He started to choke. "You made a big mistake, kid. I'm not Robin Hood, I'm the Incredible Hulk!" His eyes bulged. He began to wave his arms about wildly.

"Perhaps we made an error," said Clarice. "Let's go!"

The three girls leaped onto their bicycles.

Brick dropped his bicycle and danced around the furious teenager for a further few seconds to make sure the others got safely away, and then he followed, pedalling easily, unaffected by the swift retreat.

They didn't stop until they reached headquarters, where the girls collapsed, exhausted. "That was a narrow escape," puffed Clarice. "He nearly attacked us, I don't know why. All I wanted was to ask a couple of Incisive Questions. But he was so upset! Teenagers are mentally unstable, this proves it. Is everyone OK?"

"That was fun," said Moonflower.

Sadie groaned. "Your hunches, Clarice."

"Well, that wasn't exactly a Hunch," said Clarice. "A Good Leader must sometimes make Swift Decisions. Maybe I was a little too hasty though," she admitted. "We're sure to make a mistake now and then. But good work, everyone! Good Teamwork! Let's get an early start tomorrow with a brainstorming meeting. Bring bikes. In the meantime, try to come up with some bright ideas. Tomorrow is Tuesday, and two days to Christmas. We've got to catch that chocolate thief!"

Chapter 10

Tuesday was grey and cold. Clarice sat in the Agency office, her jacket zipped up and her yellow tuque pulled down over her ears.

Sadie arrived on her bicycle. Upstairs in the house someone was yodelling. "What's that awful noise, Clarice? I could hear it down in the Creek. Sounds like meltdown at a nuclear power plant."

"Very funny, Sadie, but you don't have to live with it."

Brick arrived next. He swooped like a hawk through the gate and slid casually off his bicycle, allowing his obedient machine to park itself as usual with a gentle bump against the Agency office. Although he seemed to have recovered some of his old acrobatic smoothness, it wasn't quite the same somehow. His heart wasn't in it;

his performance lacked lustre.

Clarice greeted him. "G'morning, Number Three. Moonflower should be here in a few minutes and then we can start. She's doing her exercises."

"What exercises?" said Sadie.

"Horsefly exercises," explained Clarice. "Moonflower and her mother do them every morning. Aunt Esther makes her. They stand at the open window and do this breathing routine. Then they gargle with salt water and they sing."

"Sing?" said Sadie. "That explains those gruesome noises."

"I told you my Aunt Esther was loopy."

Sadie said to Brick, "You look terrible, Number Three. Did you have trouble hunting down your breakfast?"

Brick shrugged.

"Still — er — packing?" said Clarice.

Brick nodded. He tried to grin, but it didn't quite come off.

"Hello, everyone!" It was Moonflower. "Isn't it a beautiful morning!"

The others looked up at the cold grey sky. They looked around at the bare branches of the trees. They looked at one another's cold faces.

"Beautiful," they agreed without enthusiasm.

Once they were settled in the office and as comfortable as the temperature would permit, Clarice said, "Let's brainstorm."

"I'll begin if you like," said Sadie. "Clarice, if your Robin Hood theory is correct — and I think it is — then it follows that our thief doesn't keep the stolen articles for himself."

"He gives them to the poor," said Moonflower happily.

"Right," said Clarice.

"Where do they live, the poor kids?" said Moonflower.

"A lot of them live in Railtown," said Sadie, "over on the other side of the Creek. As I was saying, if the Green Bandit has yet to give the stolen stuff to the poor, then he has only a couple of days left to deliver it all."

"You're right, Number Two," said Clarice. "Time is growing short. If we're ever going to catch him, then it must be soon. Any ideas anyone?"

"Probably the best idea," said Sadie, "is to split up into pairs and keep patrolling on our bikes. We think he wears green. Eventually we should spot him."

"Anyone else?" said Clarice. "No? I think your Plan is a sound one, Number Two, but first I'd like to try out a Hunch."

Sadie groaned. "Your hunches . . ."

"I'd like to follow up on the chocolate-wrapper clues," said Clarice. "They've already given us the thief's Motive. If my Hunch works out they might also Reveal his Identity."

"What's reveal identity?" said Moonflower.

"Discover who he is," explained Sadie.

"My Hunch," said Clarice, "is that the thief is a kid who buys his bars in the same area where the Crimes were committed. The big shop in the Creek is Wong's Grocery in Leg-in-Boot Square. I thought if maybe we checked Wong's they might be able to tell us who buys a lot of Robin Hood bars. What do you think?"

They considered the idea. Sadie said, "We already know that Rebecca Wood and what's-her-name, Priscilla Charles, buy them somewhere. But they're both victims."

Moonflower spoke up. "But couldn't he buy them someplace else, not just Wong's?"

"Moonflower's right," said Sadie. "There's Handy Market at the other end of the Creek at Fountain Way, or he could have bought them at any of a dozen places up the hill in the Fairview Mall."

"I've thought about that," said Clarice, "but most kids buy their stuff at Wong's."

"That's true," agreed Sadie. "The man at

Handy Market is a real grouch, everyone knows that. A kid wouldn't buy his candy there unless he needed an emergency candy fix."

"Any other ideas?" said Clarice. Nobody spoke. Brick on his potato sacks seemed to be dozing.

Then Sadie said, "Why are you so certain that the thief is a kid?"

"I'm not certain of anything," said Clarice, "but we've got to start somewhere. Which is why it won't do any harm to follow my Hunch."

Sadie said, "OK. Let's follow your well-reasoned 'hunch,' Clarice."

"Here's the Plan, then," said Clarice. "We ride over to the Creek, keeping a sharp eye out for anyone wearing green . . . "

"No joggers, please!" said Sadie.

" . . . and we check Handy Market just in case. Then we ask some Incisive Questions at Wong's, OK? Let's go."

Brick led the way over the Alder overpass into the Creek, zooming downhill like a low-flying jet. They parked their bicycles outside Handy Market. Clarice marched boldly up to the unhappy-looking man behind the counter. There were no other customers in sight.

"Good morning." She flashed her ID card. "I'm Clarice O'Brien of the O'Brien Detective

Agency and these are my colleagues." She waved an arm at her friends.

"Humph!" said the man, scowling at Clarice.

"We need your assistance in catching a Desperate Criminal," said Clarice. "Can you tell me if you have a regular customer who buys a lot of these Robin Hood bars?" She pointed to the bars displayed on the counter.

"No, I can't," the man growled.

"Surely," said Sadie sweetly, "you would notice such a person? Someone young? Buys maybe three or four bars each time?"

"Look!" growled the shopkeeper. "They come in. They buy. They pay. They leave. Which is what I advise you kids to do right now." He turned his attention to a couple of shoppers who had just walked in and were hovering around the counter. "What can I do for you ladies today?" He smiled, flashing broken teeth.

"C'mon," said Clarice, "let's go. He's no help."

They pushed along the sea wall to Leg-in-Boot Square, parked their bicycles at the fountain, and trooped into Wong's Grocery. Mr. Wong was working the cash register for customers at the front. His daughter Lucy was unpacking and arranging broccoli at the back.

They knew Lucy from school. When she saw them approaching she stopped and gave the detectives a friendly smile. "Don't tell me I'm a suspect in your big robbery case!"

"Broccoli," said Brick.

"Everyone is suspect," said Clarice grimly. "What do you know about it, Lucy?"

"Only what I hear. Bikes and dolls and all the stuff that kids leave lying around. My friend Margaux Seeley had her cellular stolen from her schoolbag while she was hanging upside down on the monkey bars Friday after school. Her mother reported it to the police."

"Why does Margaux carry a telephone?" said Sadie.

Lucy shrugged. "Quite a few of the rich kids carry them now."

"Have you seen any suspicious characters lurking about?" said Clarice.

Lucy shook her head.

"We're looking for someone who buys Robin Hood bars. Can you think of anyone?"

"I don't work the cash much," said Lucy, "so I wouldn't really know." She furrowed her brow. "The only person I can think of who always buys the same kind of candy regularly is the lady from the travel agent's across the Square, but she always buys English mints. Let me go ask my father, he remembers stuff like that."

Brick and Moonflower began unpacking broccoli from its wooden crate and arranging it on the display counter as Lucy had been doing. "Broccoli," said Brick.

" . . . is good for you," said Moonflower.

Lucy came back. "My father remembers a girl but doesn't know her name. A little kid with glasses. Very bright. She buys Robin Hood bars and *Mad* magazine."

"Anybody else?" said Clarice.

"Only Mr. Devlin. He's a nice old man who wouldn't steal a toothpick. He likes Robin Hoods though. Usually buys one each morning with his newspaper and his baby dinner."

"Why does he buy a baby dinner?" said Sadie.

Lucy yelled something in Chinese to her father at the front of the shop. Her father yelled back.

"What did he say?" said Sadie.

Lucy laughed. "Mr. Devlin has a Ferber's baby dinner on toast every morning for his breakfast."

"Yuck!" said Moonflower.

Clarice said, "Doesn't sound like our man, but we'll check him out."

"Lives on Bucketwheel," said Lucy, "at the old folks' place."

"I guess you don't know where this *Mad* kid lives?" said Clarice.

"Sorry." Lucy shook her head.

"You've been a great help," said Clarice. "Give me a call if you see or hear anything. And we'd appreciate it if you don't say anything to anyone."

Lucy smiled. "My lips are sealed."

On the way out they stopped at the front counter and quickly found in the phone book the address of the only Devlin on Bucketwheel. "Thanks for your help, Mr. Wong," said Clarice.

"You're welcome." Mr. Wong smiled kindly.

Three minutes later the detectives were leaning on the doorbell of 115A Bucketwheel. A Christmas wreath of holly decorated the front door. Above the wreath hung a green plush leprechaun.

A tiny grey man not much bigger than Moonflower came to the door. He had bushy grey hair and a bushy grey beard that grew down to his chest. He was wearing a plain black T-shirt and olive green trousers. Around his neck there hung a chain with a huge peace symbol that came to rest on his little potbelly. On his feet he wore a pair of knitted green slippers. He stood erect and looked up at the four sleuths with blue eyes that danced with merriment.

"Mr. Devlin," Clarice began, "could we talk to you for a few minutes? I'm Clarice O'Brien of the O'Brien Detective Agency." She flashed her ID.

"Robbie Devlin at your service," said the little man with a chuckle. "The Irish are always welcome. You're just in time for the dancing. Come in, come in." He threw the door wide open and the four detectives entered.

"He's batty," Sadie whispered to Clarice.

"Sit down if you like, or dance if you like," said Mr. Devlin. "I was about to dance an Irish hornpipe when you rang my chimes, so I hope you won't mind if I carry on. You're quite welcome to join in, of course." He beamed at them.

He stood to attention in the middle of the carpeted living room with his feet together and his arms loose by his sides. Then he raised his whiskered chin and fixed his eyes on the ceiling. "Shoulders back, feet together, arms at the sides, and begin on the left foot," he intoned seriously. Then as though stung by a bee he came suddenly and explosively to life, humming and dancing, singing and hopping, with a speed and agility incredible for one so old and grey.

The three girls gaped, astounded. Brick grinned.

Mr. Devlin danced and danced to the tune of his own crackly voice, his hands never leaving his sides, his feet flashing out and his knees jerking up and down like a puppet, and his peace symbol bouncing up and down on his little pot-belly.

Brick could watch no more. He leaped up and began to dance, copying the little man's style and following his fast, jerky movements with athletic precision.

The two danced together, facing each other, their arms straight and loose, their faces serious with concentration.

"This is fun!" cried Moonflower. "Keep it up, Brick!"

Clarice and Sadie sat in stunned silence. Brick never failed to astonish them.

The dance went on for several minutes until Mr. Devlin, red in the face from his exertions, brought it to a conclusion by emitting a piercing hoot and collapsing happily onto the carpet.

"Well done, boy, well done," he chortled at Brick who had collapsed beside him. "Where ever did you learn to dance like that?" He filled his lungs with air, puffing and blowing and laughing. "You remind me of myself when I was young a hundred years ago!"

He bounced to his feet and reached for a framed photograph on the mantelpiece. It was a picture of himself, smiling and happy amid all his bushy grey hair. He regarded the portrait affectionately. "See?" he said, holding it out so the intrepid foursome could see it. Catching sight of himself in a wall mirror, he paused and patted his beard and then frowned at the portrait in his hand. "Of course I was older then, when this was taken." He put the portrait back on the mantelpiece.

The four detectives saw that on the mantelpiece there was also a wooden clock. Beside the clock were several Robin Hood bars.

"You must all come again," Mr. Devlin chuckled. "We can dance a five-handed jig." He started to show them out.

"I'd like to use your washroom," said Clarice.

"First door on your right," said Mr. Devlin, pointing.

Clarice hurried down the short hallway, opened the bathroom door and looked in. Then she turned the handle of the next door and pushed it open. It was the bedroom, neat and tidy, with a narrow bed covered with a bright green quilt. She listened. She could hear the buzz of Mr. Devlin's voice in the living room. She looked in the linen closet — sheets and towels. No stolen toys anywhere. She returned to the living room.

"Mr. Devlin," she said, "we came to talk with you about your Robin Hood bars. We have reason to believe . . ."

Mr. Devlin rushed over to the mantelpiece, grabbed several of the chocolate bars, and pressed them eagerly on his young guests. "Bring along some friends and we'll dance the Walls of Limerick. That would be a rare treat indeed." He shook Brick's hand enthusiastically. "Goodbye! Goodbye! You're always welcome! Though the O'Briens were always better snoopers than dancers." He winked at Clarice, and she jumped, startled. But before she could say anything, he was ushering them out, chuckling and nodding.

The door closed behind them with a click. They stood outside, Robin Hoods in their hands, staring at the holly wreath. The leprechaun swinging on its pin seemed to mock them.

"What now?" said Sadie as they mounted their bicycles and headed back along the seawall.

"I dunno," said Clarice, "but my Hunch is that Mr. Devlin is not our man. I couldn't see any stolen stuff anywhere."

"I'm not so sure," said Sadie. "He could be a leprechaun. They're very tricky, leprechauns."

"What's a leprechaun?" said Moonflower.

"A kind of elf," said Sadie.

Clarice looked at Sadie for a moment, and then shook her head vigorously. "If Mr. Devlin is a leprechaun," she said, "then I'm your fairy godmother!"

"Mr. Devlin is a wonderful dancer," said Moonflower.

"Hornpipe," said Brick.

"And so are you, Brick," said Moonflower.

"Yeah, not bad, Dances With Elves!" Sadie snickered.

"Thanks," said Brick.

"Stop!" said Moonflower suddenly.

"What's up?" said Clarice.

"There's a girl sitting on the seawall over there." Moonflower pointed past Stamp's Landing and past the bobbing sailboat masts in the marina. "She's wearing glasses. And she's reading *Mad* magazine!"

The girl, if indeed it was a girl, was very far away.

"That's impossible to see from here," said Sadie.

"Not for me it isn't," said Moonflower. She narrowed her eyes and gazed off into the distance. "And she's just about to unwrap a chocolate bar, a Robin Hood chocolate bar!"

"Let's go!" said Clarice.

Chapter 11

Moonflower was right.

It was a girl. She wore glasses. She was reading *Mad* magazine. And she was eating a Robin Hood.

"That's absolutely amazing," said Clarice as they dismounted from their bicycles and leaned them up against a garbage drum.

"Unbelievable!" said Sadie. "Eagle Eyes scores again!"

"Hi," said the girl with a friendly smile. "Amazing and unbelievable? You've got to be talking about me."

The detectives studied her closely. The girl looked down at herself, searching for the reason for this unusual scrutiny. She was small and skinny, had untidy light brown hair, and wore a green sweatshirt printed with the words "Beam

Me Up, Scotty" under her open maroon jacket.

"We'd like to ask you a few Incisive Questions," said Clarice.

"Like some?" The girl held up her Robin Hood bar.

"Not when we're On Duty," said Clarice flashing her ID. "I'm Clarice — "

"I know who you are." The girl grinned cheerfully. "You're the kiddiecops who are trying to hook the Creek freak who's hoisting all the childgoodies, right?"

"What do you know about it?" said Clarice.

"I figure it's someone from a shoplifting family. His parents make him go out and heist his own Christmas gifts."

"What's your name?" said Clarice.

"Terri Janz. My friends call me TJ."

"Where do you live?"

"Foundry Quay, number 838. Also a Creek freak. Have you kiddiecops got me down on your spreadsheet as a suspect or something?"

Sadie consulted her notebook. "You must know the Wakabayashis. They live in Foundry Quay."

"I didn't hoist the kid's Cabbage Patch Creature if that's what you mean," said Terri Janz cheerfully. "I figure it's aliens from outer space who mistook the doll for one of their own scouts."

She got up, ambled over to the garbage drum, and tossed her chocolate wrapper into it. "You're welcome to beam aboard my habitat, kiddiecops, and search for poached playthings, but all you'll find is comics. I'm a comic freak, so to speak."

"Do you ever imagine that you're Robin Hood?" said Clarice.

Terri regarded the question seriously. "Not Robin Hood, but I imagine I'm a Starfleet Captain, and get James T. Kirk's job on the Enterprise after he retires." She grinned. "What about you? Do you ever think you're Robin Hood?"

"Thanks," said Clarice. "We'll be in touch if we need to ask you any more questions."

When they got back to headquarters there was one message in the mailbox. Clarice said, "Another bike stolen. Fairview area."

Sadie added it to the list.

"What did you think of Terri Janz?" said Clarice.

"Could be the thief," said Sadie, "but I doubt it. She's a friendly, crazy sort of girl. And she threw the chocolate wrapper away, didn't save it to use as a calling card."

"That could have been a bluff," said Clarice. "She was wearing a green sweatshirt, don't forget. Maybe we should have searched her place."

"I liked her," said Moonflower. "She was funny."

Brick said nothing. He appeared to be asleep.

"Well," said Sadie, "the chocolate-wrapper clues don't seem to have identified the bandit for us. Unless it's Terri Janz or Mr. Devlin. We could put a tail on them, what do you think?"

"Just because Terri and Mr. Devlin eat Robin Hoods doesn't actually prove anything," said Clarice. "Lots of people eat 'em without being criminals. And the wrappers by themselves mean nothing. It's how they're deliberately placed for us to find at the Crime Scenes that counts." Clarice sighed. "We're back to where we started from this morning."

"What about my idea of patrolling in pairs on our bikes?" said Sadie. "At least the wrappers told us we're looking for a Robin Hood, and if he's wearing green we're sure to spot him."

"We could do that," said Clarice, "but I just wish we had something more to go on. Robin Hood is leading us in a blind dance and there isn't much we can do about it."

"Hornpipe," murmured Brick.

"I'm hungry," said Moonflower.

"Me too," said Sadie.

"Let's bike over to McDonald's," said Clarice.

"We can brainstorm over a burger."

"Broccoli," murmured Brick.

"Wake Brick up and let's go," said Clarice.

McDonald's was crowded, but they found a quiet spot upstairs where they could look out at the silver dome of the Science Centre and the eastern end of False Creek.

"Let's review a few Facts," Clarice began once their appetites had been attended to. "First: a doll and a skateboard were stolen in the Fairview area. Today it's a bicycle, again in the Fairview area. Second: before that, all the robberies were in the False Creek area, right so far?"

"Not all," said Sadie. "Don't forget Rebecca Wood's Rollerblades in Fairview."

"Right, Sadie," said Clarice. "But except for Rebecca Wood, the robberies seem to have switched from the Creek to Fairview. So if we're going to follow Sadie's idea and patrol, then we should focus on Fairview."

"Look for Lincoln green," said Moonflower.

"Any old green," said Sadie.

 **Chapter 12**

"Clarice, I'm cold," said Moonflower.

It was two hours later. Clarice and Moonflower had been patrolling the Fairview Slopes from Oak to Cambie streets while Sadie and Brick had the west side, Oak to Fir. Clarice and Moonflower had seen nobody suspicious. They were tired and dispirited.

"OK," said Clarice looking at her watch, "it's time to get back anyway."

They pedalled wearily along 7th Avenue toward home.

"Look!" said Clarice. "There's Sadie and Brick." She pointed along the avenue where Sadie and Brick were walking their bicycles. "Wait up!" yelled Moonflower. She began to pedal quickly. Clarice followed.

Sadie saw them coming and waved her arms

at them frantically.

"Hold it, Moonflower," said Clarice, "they're following someone!"

But Moonflower plunged on. "Wait up!" she called.

Then they saw him.

He was strolling casually along, only half a block ahead of Sadie and Brick.

He was not much bigger than Moonflower.

He was dressed all in green.

He wore a green track suit and an oversized green baseball cap pulled low over his ears.

He was carrying a plastic shopping bag. The head and arms of a brown teddy bear poked out of the top of the bag.

"It's Robin Hood!" screamed Moonflower, pedalling furiously.

The green bandit started to run. He dropped the bag with its teddy bear and sprinted around the corner of Oak Street and down the hill toward 6th Avenue.

Sadie said, "Moonflower! You ruined everything!"

"After him!" said Clarice.

They pedalled as fast as they could to the corner and then stopped. There was no sign of Robin Hood.

"The back lane!" said Clarice.

They zoomed down the hill and made a fast turn into the lane. Into the alley abreast rode the four hunters.

"There he goes!" yelled Sadie as the green figure up ahead disappeared around another corner. "He's climbing up into Choklit Park!"

When the crime fighters reached the end of the lane they could cycle no farther. There was no road through Choklit Park, a small terraced square of shrubs and flowers hanging on the edge of the Spruce Street cliff. Instead of a road, seventy-three steps zigzagged sharply upward to 7th Avenue. Robin Hood was speeding up the steps. He was almost at the top.

"There he goes!" said Moonflower, her voice full of admiration for the daring bandit.

"After him!" Clarice leaped from her bicycle and started up the steps that led through Choklit Park.

The others abandoned their bicycles and reached the top in time to see Robin Hood disappear into the shopping mall.

"After him!" Clarice yelled again.

The daring crime fighters hurled themselves into the crowds of Christmas shoppers.

"Run ahead, Number Three, never mind us," puffed Clarice.

"Right, Chief." Brick was thin and fast and

could stalk his prey through the thick wilderness of shoppers like a lean jungle cat.

For a few seconds they could see his spiky yellow head bob up and down, and then he was gone. They pushed through the crowd after him. The sounds of Christmas music filled the mall. "Round yon virgin . . ." sang a choir of child angels down on the bottom level.

"I see him! I see him!" said Moonflower. She pointed down over the rail toward Santa and his helpers and the line of tiny tots with their mothers and fathers.

"All I can see," said Clarice, "is green elves."

"There! There!" said Moonflower, pointing and jumping with excitement.

"I see him," said Sadie. "He's running down the escalator on the other side. And Number Three is right behind him!"

"Let's go," said Clarice, leading the way to the escalator on their own side.

"But this escalator comes up!" said Sadie. "We can't . . ."

"Follow me!" cried Clarice.

"Down the up staircase," muttered Sadie as they rushed into the alarmed shoppers facing them on the top of the crowded escalator.

"Look where you're going!" said an angry woman in a blue hat.

"Hey!" yelled an old lady, striking at them with her umbrella. "Take the down escalator over on the other side!"

"Kids these days!" muttered an elderly gentleman as he danced aside in a stumbling pirouette.

Moonflower leaped down the upward-moving steps as she followed in the vacuum created by Clarice and Sadie. "This is fun!" she giggled.

When they jumped off at the bottom, they could see Brick chasing Robin Hood through Santa's workshop. "Come on!" said Clarice.

"Wait up!" cried Moonflower.

Clarice ran back to take Moonflower by the hand and they stumbled through Santa's workshop with its indignant elves, kicking over workbenches and tools and toys.

"Get out of here!" yelled an angry dwarf, jumping up and down and shaking his fists at them.

Up ahead, Robin Hood was trying to escape by weaving in and out between the elves and a forest of artificial Christmas trees. Brick followed easily behind, moving effortlessly, waiting to leap on his prey the way a cat waits before pouncing on the mouse it has been toying with.

"Grab him, Number Three!" yelled Clarice as she tripped over an elf's stool and collided with one of the Christmas trees, bringing it crashing to the floor. Sadie and Moonflower tumbled over Clarice's waving legs. Two more trees came crashing down.

By now, Santa himself was in a state of shock. This sudden attack on his workshop was a most unexpected development. He sat on his throne with his beard in an uproar. "Ho! Ho! Ho!" he rumbled.

Robin Hood dropped to the floor and scrambled underneath the belly of Rudolph the Red-Nosed Reindeer, peeping out of the forest. Robin's foot caught Rudolph's hoof. Rudolph trembled and tottered and crashed to the floor. To avoid being trapped under Rudolph, Brick slithered sideways like a snake. He darted underneath Santa's sleigh.

By this time, the rest of the forest was falling. Dasher and Dancer keeled over, buried under the trees. Then followed Comet and Cupid and Donner and Blitzen. Only Prancer and Vixen were left standing.

" 'Twas but two days to Christmas," chanted Sadie, "and all through the mall, fir trees and reindeers were starting to fall." She tried to get up off her knees, but her leg was pinned by a Christmas tree. "Clarice!" she yelled.

Clarice pushed the tree off her. "Sadie! Are you all right?"

Sadie scrambled to her feet and felt her leg gingerly. "I think so."

"Are you sure?" Clarice held her arm, supporting her.

"There he goes," Sadie said, pointing.

Robin Hood leaped nimbly over Vixen's back and headed straight for Santa's throne, now unoccupied because Santa was busy in the forest trying to untangle his elves and his reindeer. Vixen toppled and fell.

Brick followed. He leaped onto Prancer's back, grasped the antlers, and flipped himself in a somersault after the elusive green bandit.

The central area of the mall was by now in chaos. Horrified shoppers pushed and shoved as they sought a good spot to stand and watch the rampant destruction. Green elves and red dwarfs rushed about in total confusion.

The choir of angels sang on: "Shepherds quaked at the sight . . ."

Clarice said, "We've got him now!"

Robin Hood scrambled under Santa's throne.

Brick flew through the air as he completed his somersault.

Robin Hood emerged from the throne and jumped to his feet. Brick landed lightly beside him, threw him to the floor with a graceful scissor kick, and sat on his chest.

"We've got him!" puffed Sadie.

"Good work, Number Three," panted Clarice.

Brick pulled off Robin Hood's green baseball cap.

"Oh!" said Moonflower.

"Aha!" said Clarice.

"It's a girl!" said Sadie.

"You got me fair and square," said the girl.

"It's — " said Sadie.

" — just as I suspected," said Clarice. "But Wood isn't your real name, is it?"

"No, it's not," said the grey-eyed bandit, smiling her tilted smile. "My real name is Rebecca Hood."

Chapter 13

"All that running has made me thirsty," said Sadie.

"Me too," said Moonflower.

"I know a quiet place in the mall for thirst-quenchers," said Rebecca Hood, alias Rebecca Wood, alias Robin Hood, "and they're all on me."

"Root beer," said Brick.

"Lead the way, Rebecca," said Clarice. "I don't think we're too popular around here."

"The elves are tidying everything up," said Sadie. "They'll soon have it all back together."

"What about our bikes left in the alley?" said Moonflower.

"Safe," said Sadie. "We've got the Chocolate Thief, remember?"

Still flushed from the battle, they pushed their way through the crowd, and were soon seated behind tall cool drinks.

"Bet you wouldn't have caught me if I hadn't left all those Robin Hood chocolate wrappers," said Rebecca.

"They helped a little," Clarice admitted. "But I was on to you from the very start."

"You were?" said Rebecca.

"You were?" echoed Sadie.

"It was mostly only a Hunch," said Clarice. "When you came and reported your Rollerblades stolen, I had a Hunch you were only there to look us over."

"You were right." Rebecca smiled. "I don't have any Rollerblades. And my aunt isn't in Hawaii."

"I first became suspicious," said Clarice, "when you told me your Rollerblades were in perfect condition after 'blading on the sea wall. The sea wall that morning was all puddles after the rain the day before, so if you had been out there for an hour like you said, the 'blades would have been wet and dirty."

"Good *reasoning*, Clarice!" said Sadie.

"Also, you gave your address as 2323 Spruce," said Clarice. "There's no such number. I checked it out. The 2300 block Spruce is Choklit Park. There are no houses on that block."

Rebecca gave an appreciative nod. "I didn't

know that. But you're right, I lied; I live at 2323 Larch."

Clarice said, "At first I thought Number Two got your address wrong, but Sadie is super-reliable. She doesn't make mistakes with stuff like that."

"I don't?" said Sadie. "Well why did you go on at me like that, Clarice? Accusing me of not getting it right!"

"Sorry, Number Two, but I had to be sure."

"Humph!" said Sadie.

"Lied about my age too. I'm not eight, I'm ten," said Rebecca.

"I figured as much," said Clarice. "You're a small kid, but you acted too old for eight. I guessed you gave us a phoney name too. So I didn't know your real name or where you lived, or even what class you might be in at school." She turned to Sadie. "The phone book was no help. So we couldn't put a tail on her."

"You almost had me with that stake-out," confessed Rebecca, "but I knew you were hiding. I could hear you talking. I never enjoyed stealing anything so much as that doll." She laughed.

"Sleepy Susan," said Clarice, nodding. "You were hard to catch. For a while there I didn't think we would. But you helped us by wearing green. You could say you overdid the Robin thing."

Rebecca gave a tilted grin. "Didn't think you'd catch on."

"There was one other little giveaway," said Clarice. "You took a Robin Hood bar from your pocket, which was nothing in itself; but then you tried to hide it, saw us watching, and changed your mind."

"I noticed that," said Sadie.

"So when you add up all the evidence," said Clarice, "it had to be you, Rebecca."

"You're pretty good detectives, I gotta say that," said Rebecca.

"Thanks," said Sadie.

"Was Robin Hood your grandfather?" said Moonflower. "You have the same name."

Rebecca laughed. "My great-great-great grandfather maybe. Who knows?"

"Rebecca, did you do it because you love danger?" asked Moonflower eagerly.

"It was exciting," she admitted. "But I saw that Robin Hood movie, and the very next day I saw all these poor kids on TV. They had nothing for Christmas. That's what gave me the idea."

"Did you give everything to the poor?" said Moonflower.

"Not yet, but I'm planning to do it on Christmas Eve."

"Stealing is a Crime," said Clarice. "You can't just go around helping yourself to other people's stuff, Rebecca."

Rebecca said, "But what about the poor kids? Who buys them toys for Christmas? Nobody, that's who!"

Sadie said, "That's where you're wrong, Rebecca. First of all, Santa Claus . . ."

Clarice gave a patient sigh.

Sadie continued. ". . . whose real name is St. Nicholas, never leaves anybody out, especially if they're poor. Second of all, haven't you ever heard of Toys for Tots? It's the toy drive the radio stations and lots of other people run for poor kids every year."

"Sadie's right — about most of that," said Clarice. "You didn't need to become a criminal."

Rebecca's face fell. "I didn't? But I thought I was doing a good deed just like my hero, the real Robin Hood." She looked as though she were about to cry.

Moonflower patted her gently on the shoulder.

"You ought to give those toys back," said Clarice.

"But how can I do that? I don't remember all

the places I stole them from."

"We have a list of stuff reported to us," said Clarice. "We can give you a copy. We can even help you return them."

"I don't know," said Rebecca doubtfully. "I had my heart set on it."

"If Robin Hood were alive today," said Sadie, "he wouldn't need to steal. He'd be helping everyone with the environment instead, especially the forests. Keep Sherwood Green would be his motto. Or he'd be fighting for better housing for the poor."

"You think so?" said Rebecca.

"Say, I've got an idea," said Clarice. "You stole from the rich kids to give to the poor, right?"

"That's right," said Rebecca.

"I bet if, instead of stealing all that stuff, you had asked the kids or their parents to donate it to Toys for Tots, then lots of them would have."

Rebecca frowned. "You think so?"

Clarice said, "Drop over to our Headquarters in the morning and we'll have that list. It shouldn't take the five of us long to take everything back and ask the owners if they'd like to donate it. Then we could help you give it to Toys for Tots. Be sure to bring the Sleepy Susan doll. I want to return that personally."

"You're a great group," said Rebecca. "Do you

need another detective?"

Clarice glanced at Brick and gave an embarrassed cough. "Not right now," she said hastily. "In any case we have our fourth detective picked out already." She turned to Sadie with a grin. "She can be our Number Four Detective anytime she's in town, right, Number Two?"

With a straight face, Sadie said, "You must mean that kid from Horsefly."

"Me!" said Moonflower. "You mean me, Clarice?" Her face shone. "Wait till I tell my Daddy! And what will the other kids say when I get home? Number Four detective! Wow!"

Chapter 14

"It's snowing!" cried Sadie joyfully.

She stomped her boots enthusiastically at the entrance of the Agency headquarters. It was Christmas Eve. Sadie was ecstatic. "It will be the first white Christmas I've ever seen!" She shook the snowflakes from her tuque and her long hair. "The first in my entire life!" She leaned into the garden shed. "Hi, Rebecca."

Rebecca was sorting through the stolen toys. She straightened up and smiled her tilted smile. "Hi, Sadie."

Clarice said, "You're just in time to help figure where this stuff belongs, Number Two. I thought we might deliver it on our bikes — except for the big stuff. We could ask Number Three to return snooty Priscilla's bike."

"And collect the fifty," Sadie reminded her.

She looked around. "There's a lot of stuff."

Clarice pointed to the desk. "Say hello to Sleepy Susan."

"Has she made a rude noise?"

"Not yet. I just hope she doesn't wet on the desk before we can get her back to Amy."

Sadie looked over at the sacks of seed potatoes. "It won't be the same around here after Brick goes."

"He goes Monda," Clarice explained to Rebecca with a sigh.

"Where's Moonflower?" said Sadie to change the painful subject.

"Hospital. Should be here soon. She's going back to Horsefly Monday, too." It was Clarice's turn to change the subject. "You got all your Christmas shopping done?"

"Of course. Just one trip to Cottage Books does the trick. I get everyone a book."

"A book!" Clarice shuddered. "I still haven't read the one you gave me last Christmas."

Sadie said, "Are we open for business tomorrow?"

"Afternoon only. I'm expecting a big Case."

"What?" said Sadie. "On Christmas Day? Is the Grinch planning another heist?"

The door flew open. It was an excited Moonflower with snowflakes on her nose and eyelashes. "Happy Christmas Eve, Clarice! Happy Christmas Eve, Sadie! Happy Christmas Eve, Rebecca!"

"All OK at the hospital?" said Clarice.

Moonflower was so excited she could hardly speak. "Remember I told you I asked Santa for two very special things for Christmas?" Without waiting for an answer, she rushed on. "Well, one of them came already, and it's only Christmas Eve!"

"What is it?" said Clarice and Sadie together.

"I asked Santa to make my Daddy well again. And he did! Today, the doctor said Daddy is going to be fit as a fiddle! That's what she said. 'Fit as a fiddle!' Doctor Watterson said my Daddy will be fit — oh, isn't it wonderful?" Moonflower sparkled like a diamond. She rushed over and hugged Clarice. Then Sadie. Then she hugged Rebecca. "Where's Brick? I've got to tell him what Dr. Watterson said."

"Late as usual," said Sadie. "Probably never seen snow before. The unfamiliar landscape has him baffled. Lost in the Barrens. Not a bit like the jungle."

"Here he comes now," said Clarice, looking out the window on the door.

Sadie stood on her toes to see. "He looks like a starving snowman."

Brick's bicycle hit the shed with a muffled bump. They could hear him stomping and shaking the snow off himself. Then he burst in like a snowstorm, hands flashing, feet whirling. "Aieee!" he shrieked.

Moonflower rushed to him. "Oh, Brick! My Daddy will be fit as a fiddle, the doctor says so! Isn't it wonderful!"

Brick's face wore a happy grin.

Moonflower hugged him. "It's a gift from Santa Claus! It's what I asked him for, the very most important thing in the whole world!"

Brick's grin grew wider.

Clarice said, "You're just in time to help return some of this stuff, Number Three. Don't forget we gotta ask for toy donations for Toys for Tots."

"So how come you look so happy, Number Three?" said Sadie. "Did the mall offer you a job as a skeleton in next year's Halloween display?"

"Not going back," said Brick.

"After all the destruction we caused, who could be surprised?" said Sadie. "We wipe out the whole Christmas display — "

"Not to mention me," muttered Rebecca ruefully.

"Number Three isn't talking about the mall,"

said Clarice. "He means Africa, don't you, Brick?"

Brick nodded.

"You're not leaving!" Moonflower threw herself at Brick in another hug. "I knew it! I knew it!"

Sadie was so happy she forgot to be sarcastic. "That's the best Christmas present of all!"

Clarice collapsed into a chair with a sigh of relief. "That's wonderful, Number Three! How did you do it?"

Brick shrugged. "My Dad quit."

"Quit his job?" said Sadie.

"He'll find another one," said Brick.

"I knew it!" said Moonflower again. "Brick, you were my second very special Christmas gift I asked Santa for!"

Brick's amber eyes glowed.

Moonflower was speechless again. She kept nodding her head excitedly. At last she said, "I asked him to let you stay here with your friends. I want you to be here whenever I visit Clarice. That was my second very special wish and the second very most important thing in the whole world."

Brick grinned.

Sadie turned to Clarice and Rebecca. "That proves once and for all — Santa Claus is for real. I told you so."

Clarice shrugged. "I'm still not convinced. What did you ask Santa for, Sadie?"

"Me?" said Sadie in surprise. "Why, a white Christmas, of course!"

James Heneghan is a retired school teacher — *and* a former police officer, fingerprint expert and photographer. Whether in the classroom or on the streets, his experience in crime gives him lots of ideas for mystery writing!

James Heneghan lives in B.C., close to the famous Stanley Park. His books with Scholastic are *Blue, The Case of the Marmalade Cat* and (with Bruce McBay as "B.J. Bond") *Goodbye, Carleton High*. He is also the author of *Promises To Come* (General).

BSSU

PRINTED IN CANADA